2

"TOO SMART" JONES and the Buried Jewels

A GILBERT MORRIS MYSTERY

MOODY PRESS
CHICAGO

All Scripture quotations, unless indicated, are taken from the *New American Standard Bible*, © 1960, 1962, 1963, 1968, 1971, 1972, 1973, 1975, 1977, and 1994 by The Lockman Foundation, La Habra, Calif. Used by permission.

ISBN: 0-8024-4026-6

3 5 7 9 10 8 6 4 2

Printed in the United States of America

Contents

1

A New Mystery

"Captain Gordon to weapons control. Alien ahead off the port bow! Laser beams all on ready!"

Juliet Jones—often known as Too Smart Jones—had just enough time to straighten up. She had been planting petunias on the side of a steep hill. Suddenly she was struck in the back of the legs and thrown violently backward into the lap of a boy seated in a wheelchair.

"Flash, you crazy thing! Stop!"

Flash Gordon, whose real name was Melvin, held Juliet around the waist. "You're now the prisoner of Capt. Flash Gordon on board the starship *Enterprise*."

The wheelchair bumped down the hill. Juliet struggled to get loose.

Flash couldn't walk but his arms were

strong from pushing himself around. He held Juliet tightly and just laughed as the wheelchair rolled over the green grass.

"How do you like this, Too Smart? It's better than planting petunias."

Juliet kicked and screamed, but Flash's arms held her tight.

Then he yelled, "All hands alert! We're going for a ducking!"

Juliet looked ahead. They were headed straight toward the small stream that went around the city park. "We're going in the creek! Turn me loose, Flash!"

"Never fear! Flash Gordon is here!"

The wheelchair hit the water. It bobbed wildly over the stony creek bottom. It came to a stop right in the middle of the stream.

"There. I told you." He was grinning. "You're always safe with Captain Gordon."

Juliet pulled herself away and stood up, knee-deep in the water. "Now, look what you've done!"

"Why, I gave you a ride. That's what I've done." Flash had red hair and green eyes. He had on a T-shirt with "Gulf Shores, Alabama" written across it. He had been hurt in a car accident, but he was always doing daring things.

Juliet splashed out of the water and stamped her feet. The water squished in her Nikes. She glared at Flash. "You're crazy! Do you know that?"

Flash put his hands on the wheels and rolled his chair out of the stream. "Come on, now. Wasn't that fun?"

"We're supposed to be planting flowers!" Juliet said, pouting. "Not having fun."

Just then the rest of the boys and girls from the homeschool support group came running down the hill. Most of them were laughing. They must have seen what had happened.

Billy Rollins got there first. He was ten and big for his age. He laughed at Juliet. Then he winked at Flash. "Why didn't you throw her in the creek?"

But Jenny White, Juliet's good friend, asked, "Are you all right?" She was nine years old and very shy.

"Oh, I'm all right," Juliet said. She looked at her brother, Joe. "And what are you grinning about?"

"I'm like Billy. I was hoping Flash would dump you in the creek."

Chili Williams was an African American boy. He was wearing a pair of cutoffs and no shoes. His large ears stuck out. He was called "Chili" because he liked to eat chili so much. His white teeth flashed against his dark skin.

"I wouldn't mind doing that. Why don't you get out of there, Flash, and let me ride awhile?"

"Sure," Flash said. "Push me up the hill, and you can ride."

Chili yelped and grabbed the handles. Then he shoved the chair back up the steep hill. He was so strong that he pushed it easily. At the top, he set Flash on the ground. "Now you watch what *I* do," he said.

"Do a wheelie!" Flash said.

Chili jumped into the wheelchair. He shoved it off and went rolling down the slope. The bright aluminum wheels flashed in the sun. Chili turned right and then left. He almost upset himself. Then he came to the creek. The wheelchair bounced and threw him headfirst into the water. But he came up laughing. He yelled back up the hill, "That was a good run!"

"Bring it up. I'll take another fly at it!"

"No, you won't!" Juliet said sharply. "We're supposed to be planting flowers and pulling weeds for our community project."

The Oakwood support group was made up of children who were being homeschooled. They had decided that their project this spring would be improving the community park. They had been busy all morning.

But Juliet saw that they were ready for play now and not for more work.

"We've had enough work," Billy Rollins said. "Let's play ball."

"That's all right with me," Joe said quickly.

"No, you don't! We've got to work another hour!"

Billy gave Juliet a shove. "Who died and made you queen? Just because you get all A's doesn't give you any right to tell me what to do, Too Smart Jones! Maybe *I'll* throw you in the creek."

"You leave her alone!" Juliet's ten-year-old brother was not as smart as Juliet. But he was very protective of Juliet, who was one year younger than he was.

Billy was bigger, but Joe was faster. Maybe Billy didn't want a bloody nose. He started back up the hill.

Juliet said, "Come on, Jenny. Let's go plant some more flowers."

The two girls went back to planting. The boys grumbled, but they did, too. After a time there was happy shouting as they mixed work and play together.

Juliet was digging with a trowel when the trowel hit something that should not have been there. "What's this?" she asked.

"What is what, Juliet?"

"I don't know. It feels hard." She began to dig again. "It's—it's some wood."

Jenny leaned closer. The others came over to watch. "What did you find?" Joe asked.

"I don't know. I'll get this dirt out of the way." Juliet dug furiously. Then she could see that it was a box about one foot square.

"Wow! I'll bet it's buried treasure," Billy Rollins said. "We can split it!"

Juliet did not answer. Billy Rollins, she thought, was the most selfish boy in the world. She dug the dirt away from the edges of the box. Then she tugged at it. The box came free easily.

"The wood's rotten," she said. "Look. There was a lock on here once, but it's rusted away."

Joe leaned over and touched the box. "Must have been there a long time. It's about to fall to pieces."

"Well, open it! Let's see what's in there!" Helen Boyd was a chubby ten-year-old.

Helen's twin, Ray, stood beside her. He looked like Helen except that he was a boy. They both had on good clothes. And neither of them liked to get their clothes dirty. While everybody else was digging, they had been playing on the park swings.

Ray reached for the box. "Let me see that!"

Joe pushed him away. "Go back and swing on your swings! You and Helen haven't done a bit of work!"

Juliet hardly paid any attention to the argument. She carefully lifted the lid of the old box. Then she gasped. "It's full of diamonds!"

Everyone crowded in close to look.

"Oh, look at that necklace!" Jenny cried. "See all the diamonds!"

"And it's got initials on it in diamonds— MRM," Juliet said.

Billy Rollins said, "All that is probably ours."

Joe stared at him, "Yours? How can it be yours?"

"Because only our family has enough money for diamonds like that."

Jeers went up from several of the youngsters.

Just then, Jenny's mother appeared. "What are you looking at?"

"We found buried treasure, Mrs. White," Juliet said.

"Yes, and we're all going to be rich," Chili said. "We'll sell it and divide up the cash."

But when Mrs. White saw the jewels, she shook her head. "No, we've got to go to the police with this. It's not ours. We'll have to find the owners."

A groan went up, but Mrs. White would not argue. "We're going to the police station right now!" She began herding the small group out of the park.

"She *would* have to come along," Billy complained. "I could buy me a motorcycle with my share of that jewelry."

But Juliet was paying no attention. She was thinking, *Oh, boy! A mystery! And I'll be the one to solve it!*

Police
Chief Bender

Juliet loved puzzles. She loved *anything* that was hard to solve. As Mrs. White and the boys and girls left the park, Juliet hardly heard their yelling and carrying on. She was thinking about the mystery.

And she also had a problem. Joe wanted to carry the box.

"Joe, just let me carry it!" Juliet said.

"No, you found it, so I get to carry it!"

Joe snatched at the box, but Juliet pulled it away.

"Joe, let her carry it," Jenny White said.

"You just like her because she's too smart."

"That's not true," Jenny said.

Helen Boyd cried, "It is too!" She was keeping close to Juliet. It was as if she was afraid Juliet would run off with the jewelry.

The argument went on about who would

carry the box. Finally Juliet said, "Here, Jenny, *you* carry it."

Jenny looked surprised. But she took the box. Then she held it tightly. It was dirty and left stains on the front of her yellow shirt.

"You'd look nice in that necklace, Juliet," Jenny said. She always thought of nice things to say to Juliet.

At that moment Billy gave Jenny a hard push. Jenny fell down. The box fell out of her hands.

"You stop that, Billy!" Flash said. "Leave her alone!"

"Mind your own business!" Billy bent over to pick up the box.

But Chili Williams was faster. Chili snatched up the box. "Yah—yah!" he said. "Try and catch me!"

"Give me that!" Billy started running, but Chili Williams stayed just out of his reach. Finally Billy gave up, red-faced.

Then Joe got into the act. Joe and Billy got into a shoving match.

"Will you two stop that!" Mrs. White said. "Now, give *me* the box."

The police station was a small, red brick building set back off the street. Juliet stayed close to Mrs. White as they went into the main part of the station.

Chief Bender was sitting behind his desk.

He got up and said, "Well, Mrs. White. Surprised to see you here."

Chief Bender was a Sioux Indian. He had been a wrestler in his younger days. He still looked like one. He had big arms and a thick neck. His hair was as black as a crow's. His eyes were bright and sharp.

The chief smiled at the parade that had come into his office. "We've never had a delegation like this before, Mrs. White. What's it all about?"

She held out the box. "It's this, Chief. The children found it buried in the park."

The chief came around his desk and took the box. "What is it?" "Open it! Open it!" the children cried.

Mrs. White reached over and lifted the lid.

Chief Bender's eyes flew open. "Well, this is some find. If these are real, they're worth as much as half of this town!"

This excited everybody. "We're gonna sell them and split the money, Chief. We'll cut you in on it," Joe said.

"Well," Chief Bender said, "there's the little matter of who these belong to, Joe. Don't you think?"

"Finders keepers," Billy said importantly.

"Why, sure," Chili Williams put in. "Look at how old that box is. It's probably been there a hundred years."

"Maybe so, but they belong to *somebody*," Chief Bender said.

"Juliet," Jenny's mother said, "tell him how you found them."

Juliet told him they had been planting flowers. She'd felt her trowel hit something. "And there it was," she said. "And I'm going to find out who owns them."

Chief Bender grinned. "Too Smart Jones solves another mystery? Well, the first thing we'll do is go out to the park. You can show me exactly where you found this."

Back at the park, Chief Bender put a string fence around the spot where the box had been buried.

"Do you think you can find out who owns them?" Mrs. White asked.

" I'm not sure. We've got limited manpower here. But we'll try our best." He opened the box again. He looked at the MRM formed by brilliant diamonds on the necklace. "MRM," he said. "I wonder who that was."

"If you knew that," Ray Boyd said rudely, "you'd know where to go."

The chief gave the boy a hard look.

They started back to the police station. On the way, a loud argument arose between Flash and Billy Rollins.

"We'll never get any of that money," Flash said. He pushed his chair along, doing better than those who had good legs.

"We found it," Billy said. "It's ours."

"It's not ours. It's somebody else's. I don't think the Lord wants us to keep it."

"Don't start preaching at me!" Billy warned. "Just because your father is a preacher doesn't mean you're one, too."

Juliet knew Mr. Gordon did preach in a small church. He was a cheerful man, and Flash was a lot like his father. Now the boy laughed out loud. "You don't deserve a reward, Billy. You haven't done anything good!"

"I've done as much as you have!"

"How many times have you been in trouble with the homeschoolers? You almost got put out last week because of that trick you played on Mrs. White."

"Aw, that was nothing!"

The arguing went on, but Juliet stopped listening.

When they got back to the police station, Chief Bender began listing ways they might find the owner.

Juliet was thinking, *I'm going to find the owner of that jewelry myself.* It was always that way with Too Smart Jones. Every time there was a mystery, she had to be in the middle of solving it.

She saw Jenny watching her. Jenny was smiling. Her best friend knew her pretty well. Then she glanced over at Joe. He was scowling at her. *He knows what I'm thinking. But I don't care. I'm going to find out whose jewels those are—all by myself.*

The thought made her feel good. She looked around the little group of homeschoolers. She was thinking, *They can talk all they want to about selling the jewelry and splitting the money. I'm going to find out who owns it. It'll be fun to look! And it might be somebody who's really very poor now. I'm going to find who it is if I have to spend the rest of the summer looking.*

3

One Mean Woman

Juliet always enjoyed dinner with her family. Her mother was a fine cook. She was also very smart. She was especially good in English and history. Her father was smart in a different way. He was in charge of putting up big buildings. He also was good at telling stories.

Today Mr. Jones sat at the head of the table and looked at the steaming roast that his wife had set before them. It was surrounded by potatoes and carrots.

"Well, wife, it looks like you've done it again."

"Done what again? Cook supper?"

"This isn't supper. This is a feast," he said. "Sit down and let's get started."

When Juliet's mother was seated, they all bowed their heads. Then they took each other's hands.

"Lord, we thank You for this food," her father prayed. "Thank You for the hands that prepared it for us. We're grateful for every blessing that You've given. Keep us remembering that every good gift comes from You. And we pray in the name of Jesus. Amen."

Just as Mr. Jones completed his prayer, Joe snatched a biscuit from the bread plate.

"Joe, you stop that!" Juliet scolded.

"Stop what?" he asked innocently. He took a big bite of biscuit.

"You keep grabbing at food while the blessing is being asked!"

"I did not. I waited until it was over. Didn't I, Mom?"

"I wasn't looking. I had my eyes closed," their mother said.

"I can always tell when the blessing's about over," Joe said. "It's always the same one." He chomped on more biscuit. "I always wait until I hear the end coming before I make a snatch at the grub."

He took a huge spoonful of creamy mashed potatoes. He plopped it onto his plate. Then he grinned at his father. "I like your blessings, Dad. They're short."

"I'm glad you appreciate them. Now, pass along the potatoes, please." Then he asked, "Well, what did you kids do today? Planted flowers in the park, I hear."

"That's right, Dad. We did, but let me tell you the exciting thing—" Juliet began.

"No, let *me* tell the exciting thing!" Joe protested.

"I found it, so I get to tell!"

"Children, stop *arguing!* What is it you found? Juliet, you first. Then Joe," their mother said.

Juliet stabbed a small carrot with her fork and began waving it about. "We were planting flowers—"

"Don't wave your food around, Juliet."

"All right, Mom." Juliet stuck the carrot in her mouth. "And while I was digging—"

"And don't talk with your mouth full," her father said.

"Well, how can I tell you about the exciting thing if you won't let me?"

"*I'll* tell," Joe said. "We found a buried treasure."

Juliet glared at her brother. "*I* was supposed to tell!"

"Wait, wait a minute. What sort of buried treasure? This another game of yours, Juliet?"

"No, Dad!" Juliet protested. She leaned forward. "We were planting petunias, and my trowel hit something, and we dug it up."

"And it was diamonds with the initials MRM on them!"

"*Joe!*"

Another argument broke out.

23

Finally, Mr. Jones said in a loud voice, "If you two can't be polite, I'll have to treat you like babies! Now, what about this jewelry, Juliet?"

Juliet told the story of their adventure. At the end, she said, "Chief Bender says he's not sure he can find out who the jewelry belongs to."

"I can't imagine what buried jewelry would be doing out there in that park." Mrs. Jones looked at her husband. "Until a few years ago, that park was nothing but a field with big trees all over it."

"And the loggers took those, so it's a good place for a park now. But you say they were *diamonds,* Juliet?"

"Yes. And I saw some onyx stones too."

"What's an onyx stone?" Joe asked.

"It's a black jewel," Too Smart Jones said. "If you had studied the lesson we had on precious stones last week, you would know that."

"Aw, who cares? You can have them onyx stones," Joe said loudly. "I want the diamonds."

"Mom—Dad," Juliet said, "I'm going to try to find out who they belong to."

"That's the police's job," her mother said. "Chief Bender will take care of it."

"I know, but I'd like to try, too."

Her dad laughed. "You can count on it—if there's any kind of puzzle around, you'll find Juliet Too Smart Jones right at the bottom of it somewhere. Oh well, what harm can it do?"

"Billy Rollins wanted to sell the jewels and split the money," Joe said. "But I wouldn't let him."

Juliet stared at him. She remembered that Joe had been perfectly willing to do just that.

"I suppose hunting for the owner is just another form of research," Juliet's father went on thoughtfully. They had finished the meal except for dessert. That was blackberry cobbler with fresh cream on top. "I don't see how it could do any harm."

"I'm not sure it's good for Juliet to always be trying to solve mysteries," her mother said. "There are other things for girls to do."

"Oh, please, Mom! I promise I'll do all my homework and my projects and everything."

At last her mother agreed, too. "All right. But if I see your grades going down, that's all of that. No more mysteries for you."

Juliet grinned triumphantly and stuck out her tongue at Joe. She had no problem with studies. They were so easy for her that she always made good grades.

After she had helped her mother with the dishes, Juliet went to the phone. "Jenny? . . . I want you to meet me at the library tomorrow morning at nine o'clock . . . . Yes, we're going to find out whose jewelry that was."

Juliet got through her homework and studying quickly that night. Then she read a mystery story. The book was written for older boys and girls, but she liked the stories because the detective could always figure out exactly who the bad guys were. She read until almost bedtime.

Then Juliet glanced over at Joe. He was working on one of his inventions. "What are you inventing this time? It looks like a piece of junk."

"You'll think junk when it makes me twenty million dollars," he said.

"Well, what is it? What does it do?"

"That's a secret. You might steal it."

Juliet got up to go to her room. Then she stopped and turned around. "Someday one of your inventions is going to work, Joe. And that's when I'll faint dead away."

The sun began shining through Juliet's window. She awoke right away, as she nearly always did. Unlike most people, as soon as she woke up she usually seemed to go at full speed. One minute she was asleep; the next minute she was fully awake.

Today she bounded out of the bed, stuffed her pajamas into the hamper, and then quickly dressed. She put on a pair of jeans and her favorite lime green shirt.

After eating a quick breakfast, Juliet was on her way to the library. To her disgust, her brother invited himself along. "Why don't you go invent something?" she asked him.

"Because I want to find out who owns that jewelry. Maybe he'll give us a big reward." Joe dug an elbow into her side. "I can use the money for some of my inventions."

"I wish Mom would let us stay at the library all day. I don't see why we have to be home by noon."

"So we can eat lunch! Who wants to stay all day in a *library?* Now, if it was a ball game, it would be different."

They found Jenny White waiting at the library door. "Hi, Jenny," Joe said. "How long you been here?"

"Not long."

"Well, let's go right in and start looking," Juliet said.

As soon as they were inside the library, Joe said gloomily, "Uh-oh. Right away we see Miss Smathers."

Miss Ida Smathers was the librarian. She was tall and thin and one of the grumpiest people in town. Juliet always thought it was sad that something as much fun as books had to be handled by someone as grumpy as Miss Smathers.

But Juliet walked up to the desk and put on her best smile. "Good morning, Miss Smathers."

"What can I do for you, Juliet?"

Juliet knew that Miss Smathers did not like her to check out books. It seemed to irritate her when *anybody* checked out a book. Maybe she didn't like gaps in the shelves. For this reason, maybe, the Oakwood library was not a very popular place.

"We want to look at old newspapers and things like that," Juliet said.

"Old newspapers? They're all on microfilm. You don't know how to use the machine."

"I do," Joe said in a loud voice. "I learned how. I can work *any* machine."

Miss Smathers looked over her glasses at him. "You're not going to ruin my machine, Joseph Jones."

"I know how to use it. Really. Mrs. White taught me. And we'll be very careful."

It took some talking, but at last the three children were sitting around the microfilm machine. They looked at the big stack of reels of film.

Joe said, "Well, wow! Where do we start?"

"I don't know," Juliet confessed.

"The only clue we have is those initials MRM," Jenny said.

"Then I guess we have to look for something in the newspapers with the initials MRM."

They started. But within an hour, Juliet said in disgust, "This will never work! We've got to find a better way."

"That's what I said in the beginning," Joe said. "Let's go get some ice cream."

They took back the reels of film to the desk.

Juliet said politely, "Thank you very much, Miss Smathers."

"You're welcome," Miss Smathers said, but she did not say it very happily.

As the three children turned away, Juliet heard her muttering something. Maybe she was saying, "At least they didn't check out any books and make gaps in my shelves."

4

The People in the Old House

Juliet was disappointed at not finding anything at the library. But she never let things get her down for long. She kept thinking about what could be done. Her mind was as busy as a hive of bees.

The support group met at the church in the afternoon. They had to get ready for a math and science contest that was coming up in a few months.

After the planning time, Juliet said, "Before we go home, there's something I want to ask you."

"What is it, Too Smart?" Billy Rollins asked, grinning. "You got some problem you can't work? I'll be glad to help you."

"It's the jewelry," Juliet said.

"What about it?" Chili asked. "Somebody know the owner?"

"No. And that's what we've got to talk about."

By now, the boys and girls were outside under the shade of some tall oak trees. Overhead, a squirrel was chattering.

"I'll bring my twenty-two next time," Flash said to the squirrel. "And that'll be the end of you!"

"Flash, pay attention," Juliet said. She liked Flash Gordon, but he could be so rattle-brained at times.

"I want us to all get together and find out who owns the buried treasure."

Jack Tanner had not been there when the treasure was found. He said, "What we want to find the owner for? I think Billy's got the right idea. Just sell the treasure and split the money."

Juliet shook her head. "You always want to do everything Billy does!"

Billy grinned. "Why not? I always do the right thing."

Jack Tanner's face got red. "It just makes sense to me," he mumbled.

Helen and Ray Boyd did not want to do anything that seemed like work. Ray said, "The chief's not going to let us have that jewelry. We might as well forget about it."

"He might," Helen said. "If nobody finds the owner. Dad says then it'll belong to the finders. And that's us."

"It's not us. It's Juliet," Joe said.

"I don't look at it that way," Helen argued. "The group found it."

"You were out on the swings!" Chili protested. "You won't get any of that money."

"My dad will get a good lawyer, and we might get all of it," Ray bragged.

"Let's stop arguing. Please!" Jenny White cried. She looked at Juliet. "What do you want us to do?"

"I want us to go up and down the different streets asking everybody if they know somebody with the initials MRM."

Jack Tanner groaned. "Are you crazy? You could go all over town and not find the right people."

Billy said, "It's a waste of time."

But Juliet kept on begging everybody to help. In the end, they all agreed. But Flash and Chili said they were going to go play basketball after they went to just a few doors.

The boys and girls started down Elm Street. This part of town wouldn't take long, Juliet thought. They already knew most of the people in the neighborhood.

But when they had gone down two streets, Ray Boyd said, "I'm going home. Come on, Helen. This is crazy!"

Juliet was discouraged too, but she did not want to quit. She turned to Jenny and said, "I just thought of something important, Jenny."

"What?"

"The families in our neighborhood are *new* families. They wouldn't remember anybody from a long time ago. Maybe it's been fifty years since they buried that jewel box."

"You're right," Jenny said. "I never thought of that, either. You're so smart, Juliet."

"I'm not very smart, or I'd be thinking a little bit more clearly. Anyway, let's try going to the *older* part of town. Maybe we can find some older people who remember somebody with those initials. I don't know anything else to do. "

The two girls walked to the older part of town. They went up and down the streets there, knocking on doors, asking about the initials MRM. At last Jenny said she had to go home.

But Juliet said, "I'm not ready to go home yet, Jenny. I want to ask some more people. You go on. I'll meet you for ice cream later." The children were all going to meet at the ice cream parlor at four o'clock.

Stubbornly, Juliet continued to knock on doors. When she came to the edge of town, she was about to go back. But then she noticed one more house.

The house looked old. It was set way back off the street. It had an iron fence around it. The fence had been black once, but now it was rusty. Then Juliet saw smoke coming out of the chimney.

"I thought that house was empty," she said to herself. "Nobody's lived there for a long time." She grew curious and walked around to the front of the place. The front gate was sagging. The yard was grown up with weeds. Some of the windows were broken out. Cardboard had been put over them. It must have been a rather fine house once, but now it was faded and weatherbeaten.

Juliet walked through the old gate and up the steps. She saw that some of the porch boards were rotting. And then she smelled something very good. It was a spicy smell. It reminded her of something that she had eaten somewhere, but she could not think what it was.

"I might as well try this last house," she said. And she knocked on the door. For a long time, nobody came. She knocked again.

Then the door opened. A girl about her own age stood in the doorway. She had black hair and dark eyes. She looked at Juliet curiously.

"Hello. My name's Juliet Jones." She waited for the girl to answer. She didn't, so Juliet asked, "What's yours?"

"Delores."

"Well, Delores, if your parents are home, I'd like to talk to them."

A young boy suddenly appeared. Perhaps he was the girl's brother.

"Hello. I'm Juliet Jones. I've just met Delores. Who are you?"

"I'm Samuel Del Rio. What do you want?"

Juliet thought that was rather rude, but she smiled anyway. "I'd like to talk to your parents."

"We don't have any parents," the boy said defiantly.

Juliet stared, not knowing quite what to say. Then she decided that the boy was just angry or hurt about something. She said, "I'm very sorry."

"But my grandparents are here," Delores put in quickly. "You can come in if you want to."

Juliet was certainly curious about this house and this family. She followed the two children into a wide hallway. The floor was made of wood. Some of the wallpaper was falling down. But at the end of the hallway, a beautiful wood stairway curved upward. Juliet could tell that this had once been a rich man's house.

Just then an old woman appeared at a door that led off from the hall.

Delores said, "Grandmother, this is Juliet Jones." Turning to Juliet, she said, "This is my grandmother."

The woman who came toward Juliet was silver haired and had a round face. "Hello," she said. "What can I do for you, young lady?" She spoke with some kind of accent.

Juliet said, "I'm just going around the

neighborhood. We're trying to find out if anyone with the initials MRM lives here."

"No. I am Maria Del Rio. My husband will be back soon. He is Ramon Del Rio. But we have no one here with those initials."

Juliet liked the old lady. "I didn't know anybody lived here," she said.

"We've just moved in," Mrs. Del Rio said. "This house—" she waved her hand around "—it belonged to my husband's family many years ago." Then she said, "We are about to have dinner. Would you come and join us?"

"Oh, no. No, I couldn't do that."

"Well, at least have a taco. Come along."

Juliet loved tacos, so she followed Mrs. Del Rio into the kitchen.

This room looked in better shape than the rest of the house. A big woodstove filled one whole wall. From it Mrs. Del Rio took a taco shell and filled it with beef and onions and lettuce. She added cheese. Then she sprinkled something from a small bottle on it. "It's a little hot," she said. "Be careful."

Juliet bit down on the taco and rolled her eyes. "That's the best taco I ever ate!"

"They're better than Taco Bell," Delores said, smiling. "My grandmother even makes the tortillas."

Juliet stood in the kitchen until she finished her taco. Then she said, "Thank you very much. I'd like to welcome you to our town."

37

Mrs. Del Rio said, "We just came. We have not found many friends yet."

"Well, you come to church. That's where to meet people."

Mrs. Del Rio shook her head. "I do not think that would be possible."

Juliet turned to go. "Good-bye, Samuel and Delores. Sometimes on Saturdays we have play days over at the playground. Maybe you could come."

Samuel scowled and shook his head, but Delores smiled again. "I'd like that," she said shyly.

Juliet left the old house and made her way back to the ice cream parlor.

She found the rest of the group already there. But no one had learned anything about MRM.

"I told you it was a waste of time," Billy said.

"I think we just need to keep at it," Jenny said. "Somebody's sure to know *somebody* with those initials."

Juliet began telling the group about the Del Rios.

Billy Rollins frowned. "My dad said some Mexicans were moving in. He says they ought to go back where they came from."

"Why don't you go back where *you* came from?" Chili asked with a twinkle in his eye.

"What do you mean, where I came from? I come from *here*."

"You didn't always. Chief Bender's folks came from here." Chili grinned.

"That's right," Flash said with a laugh. "The Indians owned this country. Now *you* just go back where you came from."

Jack Tanner shook his head stubbornly. "I say let them go back, just like Billy says." He always sided with Billy, no matter what.

Jenny usually talked very little. But now she said, "I think you're mean, Billy."

Billy paid no attention to Jenny. He kept on saying that there was no room for Mexicans in Oakwood.

While they were still arguing, Jenny suddenly said, "There. That must be the kids you were talking about."

Juliet looked out the window of the ice cream parlor. "It is. Wait here. I'm going to ask them to come in, and I'll buy them some ice cream."

"Hey, don't do that!" Billy called out, but Juliet was already gone. He stared at Jack Tanner. "Why does she always have to do stuff like that?"

"I think it's nice," Jenny said. "Juliet's always doing nice things for people."

"That's right," Flash said. "Besides, what have you got against Mexicans?"

Billy shrugged his shoulders. "They're just not like us," he said. "That's what my dad says."

As soon as Juliet came back, she introduced Samuel and Delores to everybody. The two new children were very quiet. All they did was nod. Then Juliet said, "I've got some money saved up. What's your favorite flavor of ice cream?"

"I don't know," Delores said. "I don't eat much ice cream, except at home. The kind that Grandmother makes."

"How about rocky road? Let's try that. And what about you, Samuel?"

"I don't like ice cream."

"Hey, man, you gotta like ice cream!" Flash said. "You try some of this pistachio. It's the greatest stuff in the world." He grinned from ear to ear. And somehow Flash was able to talk Samuel Del Rio into trying pistachio.

Most everybody else went back for more ice cream then. But Billy said, "I'm leaving."

Jack Tanner said, "I'm leaving, too."

The two boys got up and went out the door.

Samuel Del Rio said, "They don't like us."

"Oh, they're just soreheads," Chili Williams said. "You two like to play ball?"

Samuel brightened. "I play sometimes. Baseball."

"Hey, that's cool! You can play on my team."

Juliet said, "Let's sit down and eat our ice cream." While they did, she tried to get Samuel and Delores to talk about themselves. But they didn't want to.

"Where did you go to school last?" Flash asked.

"My grandmother, she teaches us."

"Hey, you're homeschooled!" Flash said. "That's cool. We're all homeschooled."

"Oh, that's wonderful!" Juliet said. "You'll have to join the Oakwood support group. Your grandparents can come to the meetings. We do lots of stuff."

"We do lots of *work*," Joe said. "Too much studying, I say." He had already eaten his scoop of ice cream and started back for another one.

Juliet said, "Joe, don't you eat another bite of that ice cream, or I'll tell Mom. You know what she'd say."

"You're a party pooper, Juliet!"

She ignored him. "We'd like to have you come to church, too," she said to Delores and her brother. "It's the white one right off Main Street."

"I saw it," Delores said. "We don't ever go."

"Well, ask your grandparents. They can bring you. Or we'll come by and walk with you."

Samuel said, "I don't think they'll let us."

"I know what," Juliet said. "Let's go ask

41

them right now. And we can take them some ice cream."

When they arrived at the Del Rio house with a pint of ice cream, Mrs. Del Rio saw it and smiled. She said, "Thank you! I love ice cream. And this is Mr. Del Rio."

Delores and Samuel's grandfather was a small man and rather thin. He nodded at the children. Then he bowed deeply. Juliet had never seen anybody do that before. "We are honored that you are in our house. Come inside and visit for a while. You can watch me eat my ice cream!"

It was an interesting visit. Before long, Juliet was walking in the backyard with Mr. Del Rio. He wanted to show her the garden he was starting. She told him how nice it was. Then she said, "I wish you would let Samuel and Delores come to church with me Sunday. Maybe you would come yourself."

"You go to that white church on Main Street? I don't think we believe as you do, Juliet."

"Oh, that doesn't matter," she said.

"Perhaps someday. I will talk to my wife."

"She told me that your family used to own this house. A long, long time ago."

"Yes. It was many years ago. I lived here long before you were born. Probably before your parents were born! Our family traveled a lot in those days. One year we rented out the house to people who ruined it. So it has just been standing here ever since."

"Mr. Del Rio, what happened to Delores and Samuel's mother and father?"

"It is very sad. They were killed in a plane crash."

It was very quiet in the garden. Juliet said, "I'm very sorry to hear that."

"It was the greatest loss in my life. I do not know what Mrs. Del Rio and I would do if it were not for the children. They still miss their parents very much." He turned to her then and smiled sadly. "That is why I am so glad that you came by. A little friendliness means a lot to them."

"Will you stay here long?"

"I do not know. It was our family house," he said thoughtfully. "My great-grandmother lived here. I've heard that there was a big robbery during her lifetime. All that was left of any value was the house itself. She died a few years after that. Then the family rented it out —and I told you what happened. I'm going to try to sell the place. That's why we've come back now."

Juliet said, "Maybe we could all fix up the house for you. Then you could stay."

"That is a kind heart speaking," Mr. Del Rio said. "And I am glad to see that there are still kind hearts in this world."

5

A Different Kind of Preacher

Sunday morning came to Oakwood gently and with great beauty. The sun rose and spread its beams over the town, which began waking up right after dawn. Slowly the sound of voices and of cars on the wide streets became more noticeable.

Juliet lay in bed, looking up at the ceiling. As usual, she had awakened suddenly. But this morning she just lay there thinking of many things. She spent some time thanking the Lord for all the good things that He had given her. One of the things her parents had taught her was the Bible verse that said, "In everything give thanks for this is the will of God in Christ Jesus concerning you."

Juliet smiled. She thanked God that she had parents who cared for her and for Joe.

She knew that many children did not have Christian parents.

Just then a movement outside the window caught her eye. It was the mockingbird that came almost every day. She watched him puff out his chest and throw his song into the air. Then he flew off.

"I wish I could sing like that." Juliet sighed. She had many talents, but sometimes she thought she would give them all up if she could sing like Jenny White. She thought Jenny sang like an angel.

But even as she thought this, she knew it was wrong. "God made me able to do schoolwork real well, and He made Jenny able to sing. So Jenny ought to be thankful for her voice, and I ought to be thankful for my brain."

Juliet got out of bed then and stretched. She was wearing a pair of light blue pajamas. They had white stars and yellow moons decorating them. She had picked them out herself at the department store. Now she grabbed up her towel and robe.

By the time she was finished showering and dressing, Juliet heard her mother's voice saying, as always, "Joe, if you don't get out of that bed in one minute, I'm going to dump a bucket of ice water on you!"

"Aw, Mom!" Joe's voice came muffled and whiny. "I think I'm sick. I don't think I can go to church today."

"You're going to be sick if you aren't out of that bed and downstairs in exactly five minutes!"

Juliet felt pleased with herself. *She* was up without being called. She brushed her hair. She tied it with a ribbon into a ponytail. Then she picked up her Bible and left her room.

She stopped by Joe's door and knocked on it. "Joe, dear. Are you awake yet? It's almost time for breakfast."

"You get away from that door, Juliet!"

Juliet laughed. Joe always hated to get up in the morning, and she always liked to.

Downstairs, she found that her mother had breakfast almost ready. "Can I help, Mom?"

"Yes. You can make the toast. Joe's going to be late again."

"I told him to hurry up."

Mrs. Jones shook her head. "He's not lazy. He goes like a house afire after he's up. But getting him out of bed is like raising the dead."

Juliet thought that was funny.

They finished getting breakfast on the table. Juliet made the toast. She chattered to her mother about things that she planned to do. Her mother fried the bacon and eggs.

By the time Mrs. Jones was taking the eggs out of the frypan, Juliet's dad came in. He was followed by Joe.

Joe's hair was rumpled. His eyes were half shut. He slumped into his chair. "I don't see why we have to get up before daylight to eat breakfast," he muttered.

His father looked at him. His eyes crinkled up, and he grinned. "It's not daylight. I've already run five miles."

Their father loved to exercise. Every morning he got up and put on his jogging outfit and ran, rain or shine. None of the rest of the family enjoyed exercise that much. But he did look very fit and handsome. His red hair was brushed back, and his blue eyes were twinkling at his son. "And if you go to sleep in church today, I'm going to bring in a cattle prod to wake you up."

"I think it's disgraceful the way Joe goes to sleep in church," Juliet said primly. *She* never went to sleep in church. She didn't even get sleepy. "With a preacher as good as Brother Harley, I think that anybody should stay awake."

"I never go to sleep when Brother Harley is preaching!" Joe defended himself. He took a bite of egg and bit off a piece of toast and could hardly be understood. "I like his preaching. It's the other stuff that's boring. Like announcements and stuff."

Secretly, these things bored Juliet too. She reached for the jelly. She dipped into the strawberry and jellied half of her toast. Then she put blackberry on the other half.

"I don't see why you mess up your toast

with different kinds of jelly," Joe complained. "It's gross."

"It all goes to the same place," their dad said. "Now, let's eat. We're running a little late this morning."

"I invited the Del Rios to come to church, Dad."

"That's good. I hope they do. I'd like to meet them."

"The Rollinses won't like them. Billy said we don't need more Mexican people in our town."

Mr. Jones frowned. "I hate to hear that. I'll have to speak to his dad. He probably doesn't know his son's talking like that."

"Yes, he does," Juliet said. "I heard Mr. Rollins say that himself. Billy's probably heard it from him."

"Now, Juliet, you shouldn't talk about people," her mother said. "Let's pray for them instead."

"All right, Mom. I will."

There was the usual scuffle to get everybody out into the Cherokee at the same time. But finally they started off, leaving Boris, the black Lab, barking after them.

"Boris is slowing down in his old age," Mr. Jones said as they turned onto the street.

"We've had him a long time," Mrs. Jones answered. "He's getting old and stiff."

There was silence in the car. Then Joe asked, "Is Boris going to die?"

"Well, someday he will. We really have had him a long time."

The thought of not having Boris saddened Juliet. She and Joe loved the big black dog.

As their car pulled into the church parking lot, Joe looked out the window. "Look," he said. There's the Del Rios. They're just standing there like they don't know what to do."

"I didn't think they'd be here so early," Juliet said. "And they've *all* come!" She got out of the Cherokee. "I'll go say hello. And you can meet them."

Juliet ran across the parking lot. "I'm so glad to see you here," she said, smiling. "I was afraid you wouldn't come."

"We couldn't refuse such a nice invitation."

Mr. Del Rio was wearing a shiny black suit. Mrs. Del Rio wore an old brown dress. The grandchildren were better dressed, though. In fact, it looked as if they had bought new clothes for the occasion. Just a few days earlier, Juliet had seen at Wal-Mart the dress that Delores had on.

Then Juliet turned around and said, "I want you to meet my parents. Mom—Dad, this is Mr. and Mrs. Del Rio. These are my parents," she said proudly.

The Del Rios acted uncomfortable at first. But Mr. and Mrs. Jones gave them such a warm welcome that they relaxed a little.

"We have a Bible lesson in the auditorium

for the adults," Mrs. Jones said. "You two just come with us. Joe and Juliet, you take care of your friends."

"Sure. We'll do that," Joe said importantly. "Come along, Samuel. And you too, Delores. I'll show you the way. We can all sit together in Sunday school."

Delores looked rather frightened, but Juliet gave her a hug. "It's going to be fun," she said. "You can sit by me, and Samuel can sit beside Joe."

The Sunday school teacher was good. Mr. Blanton was a young man who knew his Bible very well. He also knew how to make it come alive for boys and girls.

The lesson that morning was about Caleb. Mr. Blanton talked about how Caleb led God's people to victory over their enemies. Mr. Blanton grew excited as he talked. "And so," he said as he finished, "never give up because you may not be able to do something. *God* is able."

"I like to hear about Caleb," Joe said.

"So do I." Mr. Blanton grinned. "He was an old man when they went into the new land that God had led them to. And there was one place that was very dangerous. It had a lot of enemies in it. But when their leader, Joshua, asked who would take the dangerous place, Caleb said, "I'll take it!" And as old as he was, he won the battle. Does that teach any of you anything?"

"It teaches me something," Juliet piped up. "There's nothing that God can't do."

"You're right. If we'll give our lives to Him, He can do for us anything that needs doing."

Juliet had glanced at Samuel and Delores during the lesson. They seemed to be listening carefully. But Samuel did not get rid of his frown. *He'll get over that,* Juliet thought. *At least Delores is having a good time.* She reached over and squeezed the girl's hand. "You'll like our preacher too," she whispered.

"I never saw a preacher. What does a preacher do?"

Juliet was surprised that anyone should not know that. She said, "Why, he . . . he preaches."

"Like Mr. Blanton?"

"Well, a little like that. You'll see."

After Sunday school, Joe said, "Come on, Sam. We'll get a good seat. You'll like Brother Harley. He used to be in a motorcycle gang."

"Is that right?" Samuel said with surprise. "They're rough guys!"

"I guess some of them are. But Brother Harley doesn't say much about the rough stuff. Funny thing. Brother Harley rode a Harley motorcycle."

"Harleys are cool!" Samuel said. "I'm going to get one when I get big."

"Me too," Joe said. "Hey, you and me can get on our Harleys and just go roaring off."

"I'm going to get one, too," Juliet said. She was determined not to be left out.

"Girls can't do that. But I might let you ride on the back of mine. If you're good."

"And you can ride on the back of mine, Delores." For the first time Samuel smiled just a little bit. "And the preacher here *really* used to be in a motorcycle gang?"

"That's right. But he's different now. He still has a big Harley, though. He goes around sometimes and tells the motorcycle riders about Jesus. One time they beat him up when he did that."

Samuel seemed impressed.

Then they filed into church.

Juliet said, "There's your grandparents. They're sitting over there with our folks. But it's so crowded there's not room for us too. I'll go tell them we'll sit in the balcony."

Juliet went to where her parents and the Del Rios were sitting. "There's not room for us here. We're going to sit in the balcony."

"Well, you kids be good up there," her father said.

Juliet hurried back, and soon the four children were seated up in the balcony. She soon saw that neither of the Del Rio youngsters knew what was going on. She decided to explain as things went along. "First we'll have a song, and then we'll have a prayer," she began.

"You don't have to tell them. I've got the bulletins right here," Joe said importantly. He handed a bulletin to Samuel and one to Delores. "Open it up. It'll tell you what's going to happen next."

The Del Rios opened their programs, and then the church service began.

Delores leaned toward Juliet and said, "I'm glad we're up high. If Samuel and I do something wrong, hardly anybody will see us."

"Oh, you're not going to do anything wrong."

"I mean if we sit down when we should stand up or something like that."

Juliet hugged her. "Oh, that's all right. Nobody's going to notice anything up here."

The service went on. One time Juliet whispered to Joe, "Stop drawing pictures on your bulletin, Joe! Listen to the sermon."

"Aw," he whispered back, "I'm designing my newest invention. It's going to be an automatic lawn cutter. Just turn the mower loose, and it does all the work."

Juliet shushed him, and then they all listened to the sermon.

After church, they went downstairs with the rest of the people in the balcony.

Brother Harley was greeting people at the front door. When Juliet introduced her guests, he said, "Hey, good to have you. Come back anytime."

"He's nice," Delores said as they left the building.

Joe nodded. "He's real cool."

Delores whispered to Juliet, "I like your church."

That made Juliet feel just great! "I'm glad, Delores. Now we can be in church together and in the same homeschool support group too!"

6

The Volleyball Game

The Oakwood parents who homeschooled their children met once a month. Dads and moms and children too got together in the small auditorium of the church the Joneses attended. There were ten families. Some of them even lived in other towns. But all came together to talk about plans that would involve the entire group.

Juliet sat beside Joe. She kept looking around.

"What are you looking for?" Joe demanded.

"I was hoping the Del Rios would come."

"Samuel said his grandparents won't come."

"I wonder why not."

Joe stared at her. "You're not as smart as I thought you were."

"What do you mean?" Juliet demanded.

"How am I supposed to know why they won't come?"

"Did you ever see the clothes that Mr. and Mrs. Del Rio wear?"

"Why, sure. I saw them in church."

"Well, if you saw them, then you'd see how worn out they were. I'll bet they're the only nice clothes they got—and they're not very nice. Maybe they feel ashamed of their clothes."

Juliet suddenly felt terrible. "That's right, Joe. I never even thought of that."

"Well, *I* thought of it. I bet they felt ashamed at church too."

"I guess you're the one who's Too Smart Jones. Not me," Juliet whispered. "We've got to do something."

"What kind of something?"

"I mean we've got to get them some nice clothes."

Joe stared at her in astonishment. Then he shook his head. "You are *not* smart, Juliet! You can't just go up to people and give them clothes. You'd insult them."

Juliet hit her forehead with her fist. "That's right, too. What am I thinking about?"

The school meeting went on and on.

But all Juliet could think of was how to get some nice clothes for the Del Rio grandparents. Joe was right, of course. She understood that. *You can't just march in and say, "Your*

58

clothes aren't very nice. We're going to buy you some new ones." I'll have to talk to Mom about it. Maybe she can figure out a way to help.

The meeting was long for there were many plans to be made. Besides, Mr. Boyd was in charge of things. He was a short, fat man with a round face and gray hair. Juliet always thought he seemed bossy.

"Well, we've got a lot of work to do that the children don't need to be involved in," Mr. Boyd said. "Why don't we let them go outside and play some volleyball while we get the work done?"

Everyone agreed to this, no one more happily than the youngsters themselves! They stumbled out of the small building, and soon a lively volleyball game was taking place. As usual, Billy Rollins and Jack Tanner were running everything. They had managed to get most of the older children on their side.

Flash Gordon came a little after the game started. "Hey," he said, "I want in this game."

"You can't play. Not in a wheelchair."

"That's what you think!" Chili Williams said. "Why, me and Flash can beat you and your bunch all by ourselves."

Billy Rollins laughed. "In a pig's eye!"

Jack Tanner laughed as an echo of Billy's words. Then he said rudely, "Get off the court so we can play!"

But Flash Gordon said, "Chili and I and

Juliet and Joe *can* beat all the rest of you. If we don't win, we'll do all the cleanup after the meeting."

"That's a bet!" Jack Tanner laughed.

"It's not a *bet*." Flash shook his head. "Anyway, I don't bet. None of us do. But we can beat you."

"Call it whatever you want," Billy yelled. "We'll even let you have first serve."

Almost as soon as the new game started, Juliet saw that Chili and Flash had practiced. And she knew that they *could* win.

In the first place, Flash had a serve that almost nobody could return. He did not have to be on his feet to serve. Billy and Jack soon found that out.

Flash rolled his wheelchair to the corner of the court and hollered, "Ready?"

"Let's get this over with!" Billy yelled back.

Flash turned his chair sideways to the net. He held the ball in his left hand and drew his right arm back. When he hit the ball, it went flying like a bullet. It was traveling so hard it nearly knocked Billy down. All Billy could do was bat it away.

"One for our side!" Chili cried. "You guys give up?"

Jack Tanner was a good player, but Juliet heard him tell Billy, "His serve is going to be hard to beat."

Billy Rollins hated to lose. "We'll beat 'em! Watch out now!"

Flash got the ball back. He said, "Here it comes. Get ready." He served again. This time the ball went just as hard. Jack Tanner got a hand on it but could only knock it into the net.

"You guys give up?" Chili yelled again.

Juliet just stood and watched. She and Joe and Chili had nothing to do. Again and again Flash sent the ball like a speeding bullet. Everybody on the other side got farther and farther back. But then he hit the ball so lightly that it just dropped over the net. No one could get it.

Finally he served the winning point, and Billy missed it. "You're cheating!" he yelled.

"We're winning, not cheating!" Flash said. "Come on, Billy. Let's play another game."

But Billy Rollins stomped off, followed by Jack Tanner.

"He sure is a poor loser," Joe said. Then he grinned at Flash. "That's the best serve I ever saw."

"Yeah, but we practiced it a lot—Chili and me."

Chili Williams's face shone in the sunlight. "We're thinking of going professional," he said.

"I'll tell you what," Flash said. "Let's play a game now where the *little* kids can have some fun."

Flash was always that way, Juliet had noticed. He was always thinking about others. "I'll help, Flash. What do you want to do?"

For some time they kept the smaller children entertained. But then Mrs. Boyd came to the door and called them all in.

When they were inside, Mr. Boyd said, "We're planning a school picnic for next Saturday at the community park."

Everybody cheered. They always had a good time at picnics.

"I'll organize a volleyball team, too," Flash called out. He looked at Billy and said, "Billy, you get a team together. We'll have a good game."

Billy's face clouded over. He said, "Who wants to play that dumb game?"

Billy had been beaten by a boy in a wheelchair, Juliet thought. He was angry and hurt and humiliated.

He said, "And keep those Mexican kids away from our picnic! Who needs them?"

Silence went over the room, and Billy's father said hurriedly, "Now, Billy, this is no time to talk like that."

"Well, that's what you said, Dad!"

Mr. Rollins's face grew red. For once, he seemed to have nothing to say.

Juliet and Joe's dad stood up. He said, "I would like to say something. We're all in this business of homeschooling so that our children will get a better education. We want them to learn more than how to read and write. We're all homeschooling because of values. And one of the values that I'm interested in is loving our neighbor.

"Our pastor preached on that last Sunday. A neighbor is anyone we meet who has a need. The Bible is clear on that. We're to love everyone, regardless of what they look like or what they are like. Jesus did. And I want to say that I will welcome the Del Rios at our picnic, or in my home, or in my church."

People clapped, and again it seemed Mr. Rollins could think of not a single thing to say.

Juliet was very proud. She was glad that she had such a fine father.

7

Dressing Up

Juliet and Jenny were working on their lessons together. Jenny had a hard time with numbers, so Juliet had agreed to help her. They had been at it for more than an hour.

Jenny shook her head. "I think that's about all my head will take today."

"All right. Why don't we quit, then? You're doing OK, Jenny. You're going to be a whiz at math when I'm through with you."

Jenny shook her head again. "I just don't see how you do it, Juliet. You just look at a problem, and you know what to do."

Juliet shifted uncomfortably. She knew that at one time she had been proud of being smart. But she had learned a few hard lessons. One of them was that being smart is not as important as being kind.

And she knew that Jenny White was probably one of the kindest girls she knew. Jenny was never angry with anyone, it seemed. Juliet at times had to keep a firm hold on her temper.

Jenny suddenly said, "I know what let's do."

"What? Get something to eat?"

"Not right now. Let's go over to the Del Rios. We can invite them all to the picnic."

"They already have an invitation. Mom sent them in the mail. To all of the families."

"I know, but I'd like to give the Del Rios a special invitation. Mr. and Mrs. Del Rio didn't come to the meeting, and I've been thinking about them. Maybe they didn't feel welcome."

Suddenly Juliet realized that Jenny was right. "That's a good idea, Jenny. And we can tell them that at picnics everybody just wears the oldest clothes they have."

"That's right!" Jenny said excitedly. "Let's go over there right now."

They told their mothers where they were going and soon were walking up to the Del Rio house. They could see Delores playing in a tire swing. Samuel was pushing her and spinning her around and around.

"That looks like fun!" Juliet called to them. "Can I do it?"

Samuel turned to her and said, "It'd probably make you sick."

"No, it won't," Juliet said. "Let me try it."

"Not me," Jenny said. "I don't like to get dizzy."

Delores got off and Juliet climbed into the swing. The tire was tied with an old rope to the limb of a tall walnut tree.

"I'm going to give you a good ride, Juliet." Samuel winked at Jenny. "Here we go!"

Samuel began to push the swing. Soon it was going in a wide circle. Then he grabbed her feet and spun her as hard as he could.

Juliet loved rides at carnivals, and this was a little like one of those. But Samuel was spinning her so fast that she did begin to get dizzy. "Not so hard, Samuel. I'm getting dizzy."

"I thought you wanted a fast ride!"

"Not this fast. Let me off!"

"Stop her, Samuel!" Delores commanded. "She might get sick."

"OK. I will." Samuel grabbed Juliet's feet and pulled the swing to a stop. He grinned at her. "Just let me know if you want another ride."

Juliet got off the swing, and for a moment the world seemed to be going around. But she laughed. She said, "We ought to get a job with the carnival with this. That ride made me dizzier than any of theirs do."

"Are your grandparents home?" Jenny asked them.

"Yes. Come on inside. Did you come to see them?"

"Well, we finished studying, and we thought we'd come over and see what you were doing and—"

Samuel said, "I've got to go to the store. Don't want to play with a bunch of girls." He went off.

"Why are boys so silly?" Jenny asked. "Nobody would make fun of him for playing with us."

"I don't know, but boys are just like that," Delores said.

Juliet said, "I wouldn't mind playing with three *boys*."

In the house they found Mrs. Del Rio making tortillas. She beamed at her visitors and said, "Oh, I'm so glad you've come over, Jenny. And you too, Juliet. We'll have some fresh tortillas for you after a while."

"I love Mexican food!" Jenny said. "I get Mom to take me to the Mexican restaurant every chance I get."

Mrs. Del Rio seemed pleased to hear that. "For a long time I was a cook in a fine restaurant in San Antonio."

"I wish you'd teach my mom how to make some of your favorite things," Juliet said quickly. "All of us like Mexican food."

"I will be glad to. You tell her to come anytime, and I will teach her."

Just then Mr. Del Rio came in through the backdoor. He greeted the girls. Then he said, "I am working in my little garden. But I'm glad to see you."

Mrs. Del Rio said, "Delores, why don't you show the girls around the house?" She added, "It was once a fine home. I'm afraid it's too late for that now."

"I hate to see the house sold," Mr. Del Rio said sadly. "I remember spending many happy days here when I was a boy. It's been in the family a long time. A long time."

"Isn't there *any* way you could keep it?" Juliet asked. "We'd like it if you stayed here."

"The house is not safe to live in, I'm afraid," Mr. Del Rio said. "Your chief of police came by and gave me a warning."

"Chief Bender? Why did he do that?"

"Because he says the house is not safe. And it would take a great deal of money to fix it up. So we cannot stay here very long. He is a good man, and he was sad to tell me this, but it is the truth. We must do something soon."

Juliet said without thinking, "Well, God owns all the houses in the world. If He wants you to live in this one, He can make it happen."

Mr. Del Rio looked startled. But then he said, "That is right, Juliet. God is able, but sometimes He does not give us what we ask for."

His wife turned to him suddenly. She said, "Ramon, have you too been praying that we could stay here?"

"Yes, I have. Have you?"

Mrs. Del Rio nodded, and tears came into her eyes. "It would be so nice, but I can see no way."

Mr. Del Rio said, "Delores, why don't you show the children the house?"

"It's a very big house," Delores said. "And lots of different things were left here."

The three girls started off.

Delores seemed pleased to show them around. "It's a nice old house. It's just dirty and run-down," she said.

"That's right," Juliet said. "It just needs some paint and wallpaper and some fixing up. It could be one of the prettiest houses in town."

"Do you really believe that God could let us keep it?" Delores said wistfully.

Putting her arm around Delores, Jenny said, "Of course, He could. And we'll just all ask Jesus to give this house to you and your family—if that's what He wants. He knows what's best."

"I do not see how that could be," Delores said.

Seeing that the girl was sad, Juliet changed the subject. "Show us everything," she said.

They went through all of the rooms, and Juliet was surprised at what a nice house it must have been. She began praying right then that God would let the Del Rios stay in Oakwood—if that was what He wanted.

"Now I will show you something you will like," Delores said. She led the way up a stairway to the very top of the house. "There's a light up here," she said. "My grandpa put it in so that we could see."

It was the attic—and Juliet decided that it was the best place of all. The big room was filled with what seemed to be junk—an old baby carriage with a wheel missing, cardboard boxes that were yellowed with age and were mostly filled with old papers.

Delores said, "Come and look at this." She went to a large black trunk. "Look what's inside," she said.

Jenny and Juliet leaned forward eagerly, and Juliet exclaimed, "Why, it's full of clothes!"

"All kinds of clothes!" Delores said. She looked at the two girls. "Do you know what I like to do?"

"What?" both girls asked.

"I play dress up."

"Oh, I like to do that!" Jenny said.

"So do I," said Juliet, "but I don't have any old clothes to dress up in."

"Well, we have plenty to dress up in here. Isn't this pretty?" Delores pulled out a black silk dress. It had streaks of green through it. Tiny pearls were sewn around the neck and on the sleeves. "This is my favorite. I put it on and pretend I'm a princess."

"Could I try it on?" Jenny asked eagerly.

"Sure. Here's one for you, Juliet. I like it almost as well," Delores said.

Juliet took the dress. It had once been white but was now mostly gray. But it still had sparkling stones sewn onto it. "I'm going to try it on," she said.

That was the beginning. For more than two hours, the girls pulled clothes out of the old trunk and tried them on. There were blue dresses, black dresses, green, red, and orange. Most of them were small sized. Although they still were too big for any of the three girls, they were just the thing that girls like to dress up in.

"There are these too," Delores said. She opened a tin box. Inside were all kinds of earrings and necklaces.

"How do you put these earrings on?" Juliet asked.

"They have this little thing on the back— like a screw. I guess people didn't pierce their ears back then. Here are some pretty green ones."

The three girls tried on dress after dress and exchanged the jewelry. They pretended to have fashion shows. And the time flew by. It was one of the best afternoons of Juliet's life.

The shoes were as much fun as anything else. They all had very high heels. The leather was cracked, but they were great fun to put on.

Then Juliet put on a pale green evening dress. It was made of some crisp material. She found some green earrings and a necklace to match. She even found a hat such as she had never seen before. Then she put on a pair of old black shoes with very high heels. She walked back and forth, pleased with herself.

"I wish I had a mirror. I'd love to see myself."

"There is one. Right over there. See?" Delores cried.

It was an old mirror in a wooden frame, and it was covered with dust. But when the girls had cleaned off the dust, they could see themselves from head to foot.

Then, of course, they had to try on the clothes all over again.

At last Juliet said, "Oh, this is fun, but we've got to go home."

"Can we come back and do it again, Delores?"

Delores seemed pleased to have found something her friends liked. She said, "Come anytime. We could put a table up here and have a tea party. Grandmother can make us some of her special tea and some of her cookies. We could do it right now."

"No, we've got to go home right now," Juliet said regretfully.

Suddenly Jenny laughed. "You know what?"

"What's so funny?"

"I was thinking about Samuel. It's a good thing that he *didn't* come with us. He wouldn't enjoy playing dress up."

"No, I do not think a boy would like a thing like this," Delores said. "But it's just the thing for girls."

"It's one kind of fun girls have that boys can't," Juliet said.

Downstairs the three girls found Samuel sitting on a stool, eating a tortilla. "What were you doing?" he asked. "You were laughing like hyenas up there."

"We've been playing dress up," Juliet said. "You can dress up with us next time."

Samuel scowled. "No way!"

Mrs. Del Rio said, "Sit down and eat some tortillas. Not enough to spoil your supper, perhaps, but you must have a taste."

The tortillas were excellent, and Juliet could have filled up on them. But she knew that Mrs. Del Rio was right. "I've got to save room for supper," she said. Turning to Delores, she said, "This has been the most fun I've had in a long time."

Mr. and Mrs. Del Rio looked at each other and smiled. "We are glad that you had a good time, Juliet. It is good to have friends."

Then Juliet remembered why they had come. "Oh, and you've got to promise to come to the picnic Saturday. And don't wear any nice clothes. It's not that kind of thing. We all wear our oldest clothes so that we can do anything we want to. Will you come?"

"I think that would be possible. Do you think so, Mama?"

"Yes, Ramon. We will go."

As soon as they were out of the house, Juliet said, "Well, that was a good idea you had, Jenny. I'm glad you thought of it."

Jenny was pleased. Her face shone. "I like the Del Rios. I don't see why the Boyds and the Rollinses have to be like they are."

Juliet did not see either, but she did not say anything. She was trying not to talk about people—even when they behaved as badly as Mr. Rollins. "Let's go by the police station," she said, "and see if there's any news about the treasure."

"All right. I'd like to find out myself."

Juliet and Jenny stood in front of Chief Bender, who was tilted back in his chair. "Have you found out anything about who owns the jewelry?" Juliet asked.

"Not a thing. I've had some people look at the jewelry—people who should know. But it doesn't strike a bell with anybody."

"What will happen if we don't find the owners?" Jenny asked.

"I guess it will belong to the ones who found it. And that's you, isn't it, Juliet?"

Juliet shook her head. "Those aren't my

jewels. They belong to somebody, and I'm going to find out who."

"Maybe I ought to put you on the force. Special detective in charge of finding missing persons."

Juliet liked Chief Bender a great deal. "Does it pay much?"

"Not as much as they pay me. But I'll give you a badge."

Juliet shook her head again. "I don't guess I need a badge. But I *am* going to find out who buried those jewels. And why they did."

Chief Bender grinned at her fondly. "More power to you, Juliet."

8

Acrobats

The sun was shining, and white clouds floated overhead. The fountain in the center of the pond at the park made splashing noises. From everywhere sounded the cries of children at play. The grown-ups were calling to one another and laughing .

"I like picnics," Juliet's dad said. He was standing at a grill, cooking hamburgers and watching all the activities. He was wearing a white apron with World's Greatest Chef on the front. He had a white, puffy cap on his head like the ones chefs wear on television.

"You just like to eat hamburgers." Mrs. Jones was setting the tables. "I think it's a good thing for us all just to get together like this. People don't have time to do things like this anymore."

"Well, it sure beats watching soap operas."

"Or even a baseball game?" she teased.

He grinned. "Well, I thought about bringing a portable TV out here to watch the Rangers play."

"Don't you ever dare do a thing like that! We don't need TV when we've got all of this."

There was, indeed, no need for television. Games had been well planned by Jenny's mother. At that very minute a three-legged race was about to start. Two people the same size would tie one's right leg to the other's left leg. Walking was very awkward, but Mrs. White had gotten eight contestants.

Jack Tanner and Billy Rollins were one pair.

Chili Williams chose Juliet as his partner. He said, "We can beat those two."

Samuel Del Rio and Joe formed another team. The Boyd twins would team up with no one but each other.

At last everybody was at the starting line. Mrs. White said, "There's the finish line down there. The first team to get there wins the prize. Are you ready?"

"Ready!" Billy Rollins hollered. "Let's show 'em how to race, Jack."

"Right. We can't lose."

Juliet looked down at the cloth that tied her leg to Chili's. "I don't see how we're going to do anything like this."

Chili grinned at her. "There's a secret to this."

"What is it?"

"Trying to go too fast will get you beat. You watch Jack and Billy. They're out to win, so they're going to try to run. They won't get far. And everybody will make that mistake except me and you, Juliet. It's a real honor for me to run in a three-legged race with Too Smart Jones."

"Don't call me that!"

"OK. But why not? You call me Chili, and that's not *my* name."

"But you like your nickname."

"Don't you like to be called Too Smart?"

"No, I don't."

"Then I'll try not to. Anyway," he said, "what we do is just go slow and easy. That way we don't fall down, and we win."

Mrs. White called out, "Ready—set—*go!*"

"Easy now," Chili said. "Just walk."

"But everybody's getting ahead of us already."

"They won't last long. You watch."

Juliet and Chili kept a slow, even pace, and they dropped far behind. But she soon saw that almost everyone, after going a short distance, was trying to run. Then they would fall. Billy and Jack fell twice and soon were arguing loudly and blaming each other.

"Easy does it," Chili said. "We're going to make it now, Miss Jones. Is that better?"

"Just Juliet is all right."

It worked best for Juliet and Chili to walk with their arms around each other's waist. And she found that three-legged walking was almost easy—as long as they went slow. "Look," she said. "Jack and Billy are down again."

"They're going to lose this race. And here comes the finish line."

Juliet and Chili crossed the line first. All the parents cheered—except the parents of Billy Rollins.

"And the winners are: Chili Williams and Juliet Jones!" Mrs. White handed a package to Juliet.

"Open it up. See what we won," Chili told her.

Juliet opened the package and found six Snickers bars.

Chili grinned. "My favorite vegetable."

The next event was the basketball free-throw contest. They had two contests—one for the younger children and one for the older ones.

Jack Tanner was a good free-thrower. But he had a hard time beating Flash Gordon. Being in a wheelchair did not hurt Flash's shots. The two tied and had to go into extra throws. Finally Jack won. But he looked at Flash and said, "Boy, that's a good shot you've got there. If you could just run, you—" He broke off, embarrassed. He must have realized that he shouldn't have mentioned Flash's handicap.

"Oh, someday I'll run," Flash said. "You wait and see. God's going to heal me and get me out of this chair."

"He really believes that," Juliet whispered to Delores. "He thinks God's going to make him well, and he'll be able to walk again."

"That would be wonderful," Delores said.

The contests went on, and Samuel Del Rio found himself enjoying the fun. There were even croquet and badminton games. Everyone won a prize of some sort. The prizes were not very valuable, but everybody seemed to have a great time, anyway.

Samuel was paired with Jack Tanner in one of the games. All at once he asked Jack, "Why does Billy have to be so mean?"

"Aw, he's just like that. He doesn't mean anything by it."

Samuel looked at the older boy. "I think he does. You want to watch out."

"What do you mean watch out?" Jack Tanner asked.

"I mean you're liable to get to be like him," Samuel said quietly. "People get to be like the people they hang around with. I'd hate to see you get to be like Billy."

Juliet was watching Jenny White's mother and Jack Tanner's father. "You know," she said suddenly, "they need to get married."

"Who?" asked Joe.

"Jack's dad and Jenny's mother."

"Are you crazy!"

"It makes sense," Juliet said. "Each of them has half a family. Mrs. White doesn't have a husband anymore, and Mr. Tanner doesn't have a wife. Jack doesn't have a mother. And Jenny doesn't have a dad. It would be nice."

"Sometimes I wonder about you, Juliet."

"Well, it would work."

"You don't know anything about Mr. Tanner. You don't know everything about Mrs. White, either. They might hate each other. People have to fall in love before they can get married."

Juliet was quiet for a while. Then she said, "Well, it would be nice if they would fall in love and *then* get married."

"Oh, come on," Joe said in a disgusted voice. "Let's go down and play on the monkey bars."

They walked over to the part of the park that had swings and bars to play on. Billy Rollins was on the bars. He was about to "skin the cat." He held onto a bar by his hands, pulled his legs up between his arms, and then hung upside down.

"Look at me! I bet none of you can do this. If anybody can do better than me, I'd like to see you." Then he dropped to the ground.

Delores said, "Go on, Samuel. Show him."

"I don't want to."

"Show us what?" Jack Tanner asked. "Are you better than Billy?"

"Maybe."

"Aw, you're just a talker. Go on and show me."

Samuel's face grew stern. "All right. I'll show you." He walked to a single bar that was used to chin on. He leaped up and grabbed it and began swinging back and forth, back and forth, forward and back.

"Is that all you can do?" Billy yelled. "Get off and let me show you how!"

But suddenly everybody gasped. Samuel was not just swinging back and forth. He threw his body over the bar. Then he was going around and around and around, swinging in giant swings.

And then there were screams, for Samuel flung himself off the bar! He doubled his body up, did a perfect backward somersault, and landed on his feet. Turning around, he grinned at Billy. "Now, let's see you do that!"

"And let's see you do *this*." Delores planted her feet and then threw herself backward. She landed on her hands. After that, she did a series of back flips and ended in a perfect backward somersault. She held her hands out to the side and bowed and said, "Ta *da!*"

All the kids except Billy immediately surrounded the Del Rio children. Everybody talked at the same time.

"How did you learn to do that?" Juliet cried.

"Our parents were fliers in a circus," Samuel said.

"What's a flier?" Jack Tanner asked.

"He means they did things on a trapeze," Juliet explained.

"Oh, that's the most beautiful thing in the world," Jenny said.

"Our parents were the best in the world!" Delores said quietly.

Samuel nodded. "You should have seen them. My mother would fly through the air, and my father would catch her. It was pretty."

Billy Rollins was standing at the back of the crowd. "Come on, Jack," he said. "Let's go do something fun."

"Wait a minute," Jack said. "Did you see what they did? I'd like to learn to do that."

"Who wants that? Come on!"

"You go ahead. I want to stay."

"All right, stay! See if I care!" Billy said and stalked off.

Soon even the grown-ups were standing around watching. Delores and Samuel kept everybody entertained with their acrobatics.

Juliet was listening to her dad talk with Mr. and Mrs. Del Rio.

"I've never seen anything like that," he said. "You never told us your children were so athletic."

"It is in our family," Mr. Del Rio said. "When we were young, my wife and I also were fliers with a circus. And then our son was. We taught him. We had hoped Samuel and Delores would do the same, but then their parents died."

"I was so sorry to hear about your son and his wife," Juliet's mother said. "But you have two fine grandchildren there."

Mrs. Del Rio said quietly, "And you have made life much better for us. You have found a place in your hearts for us."

"We'd like to see you stay around here," Mr. Jones said.

"I'm afraid that will not be possible. We have received an offer to buy our house."

"And then I suppose it will just be torn down. And that will break your hearts."

"These things happen," Mr. Del Rio said heavily. He put an arm around his wife. "It is as God wills."

"God is a big God," Juliet's dad said. "I know that Juliet's been praying about your problem. The other day in our family prayers she was asking God to help you keep your house."

"That would be wonderful. But sometimes what we pray for does not happen."

"There was a preacher once," Juliet's mom said quietly, "who said, 'Attempt great things for God and expect great things from God.'"

She put an arm around Mrs. Del Rio and said almost in a whisper, "We're going to believe God will do a miracle in your life, Maria. Somehow I believe He wants you to have your family here in this place. If He does, He can help you keep your house."

Tears came to Mrs. Del Rio's eyes. It seemed she could not speak Then she said, "I pray God that it will happen."

9

Flash and Chili

The hard rain erased all hopes of playing ball. To stay dry, Flash and Chili got under one of the picnic shelters in the park.

They had been playing handball. Since Flash was in a wheelchair, the two of them—they had become fast friends—had changed the rules of every game possible so that he could play it. Handball had been hard, for handball players have to move fast. Chili finally had come up with a set of rules.

"What we'll do," he said, "is this—I'll draw a line right here on the court." He pulled out a piece of chalk and marked a line. "My balls have to hit *inside* of this. But yours can hit anywhere."

"That's cool, Chili." Flash grinned. "Let's try it."

Chili was very fast on his feet, but his play

area was also very small, so he often missed it. Flash was limited by how fast he could wheel his chair around. But if he got to the ball, he had strong arms and could slam it against the wall. Since it didn't matter where his ball hit on the court, he would win most of the time.

But today after three games, they had been drenched by the rain. They sat in the shelter, watching it fall.

"I like the rain," Chili said. He reached into his green bag that had Adidas written on it in white letters and pulled out a bag of potato chips and some candy bars. "Lunch." He grinned. "Don't have any chili. Sorry."

"This will do fine."

They sat a while longer, crunching potato chips and talking and watching the rain fall. When they'd finished eating, Chili turned to Flash and said, "Does it bother you that you're always stuck in that wheelchair?"

Flash Gordon ran his hands over his dull red hair. "Sure, it bothers me," he said. "Wouldn't it bother you?"

"Yeah, it would bother me. But you never *act* like it bothers you. If I had to stay in a wheelchair, I'd be mad all the time."

Flash studied his friend. "Does it bother you being black when the rest of us aren't?"

Chili stared without speaking for a moment, then said, "If everybody was like you, I wouldn't mind being black. But everybody's not like you."

"If everybody was like *you,* it'd be a better world. You're my best friend."

Chili grinned at him. "You must want something—to say nice things like that about me." Then his smile disappeared. "You think you're going to get out of that wheelchair someday. Well, one thing's for sure—I'm going to be black as long as I live."

"The preacher says don't ever want to be something you're not, Chili. When we say, 'I want to be born different,' we're blaming God because He made us like we are."

"I guess it doesn't matter. God loves everybody the same— doesn't matter what they look like."

"Sure He does. People are the ones that think looks matter."

"I can kind of see that. But it's hard being different. I'm the only one that's black in our whole support group. Think about what it would be like if you were—"

"Well, I'm the only one in a wheelchair! And if we had somebody who was blind, they'd be the only one that was blind."

"I know." Chili picked a baseball out of his pocket and began tossing it up and down. He was very thoughtful for a time. Then he said, "I know God made us like we are. But you don't think God caused you to be in that wreck that hurt your legs, do you?"

"We don't know why He lets stuff happen. I know one thing, though. My dad always says that nothing is impossible with God. He says that doctors can say I can't walk, but God hasn't said it yet. So every night Dad comes in and prays for me to get well. Mom does, too." Here Flash smiled. "I bet if you told the truth, *you* pray for me, too."

"I sure do. Nothing I'd like better than to see you get out of that wheelchair."

"Well, I believe I will someday. It's just a matter of time. God's time."

It always made Chili feel better to talk to Flash.

Pretty soon they were talking about the buried jewels. "What do you think about that buried treasure?" Chili asked.

"I haven't thought much about it. Billy Rollins still wants to sell it and divide up the money."

"What does he need money for? His family's got enough money to burn a wet mule."

Flash's grin was wide. "Does it take a lot of money to burn a wet mule?"

"I don't know. Just something I heard my grandpa say. Anyhow, *I'd* sure like to have some of that money."

"It'd be nice to have money all right. You could do good things with it." Suddenly Flash blinked. "And I just thought of something! You know how Juliet was telling us Samuel's grandparents don't have any nice clothes?"

"Yeah. They wear the same clothes to church every time."

"I'll tell you what let's do. I've got some money saved up. Why don't we buy them some new clothes?" Flash asked.

"'Cause Juliet says we can't just up and give them clothes, that's why. We'd make them feel bad."

"They don't have to know who gave them. We could just buy 'em, and wrap 'em up, and leave 'em on their doorstep."

Chili thought about that. "Now, that's cool —that's *real* cool! How much money you got?"

"I don't know. I'll have to count it. You got any?"

"Yeah. I got a little. We could put it together. You want to tell anybody else so they can help?" Chili asked.

"No. Let's just me and you do it. Let's don't ever tell anybody. I think the Bible says if you give something to somebody like that, you do it secretly."

"Then that's what we're going to do." But then Chili wrinkled up his forehead. "But how are we going to buy clothes for old folks? I don't know anything about no grown-up clothes."

"Well, that's a problem," Flash said. "But

I'll bet we can solve it. Two guys as smart as us, we can figure it out."

"Yeah." Chili grinned. "They're going to be calling us Too Smart Gordon and Too Smart Williams. Juliet Jones has done lost her name!"

"We're going to do what?" Joe asked.

The home school students were together for their weekly meeting. Even the Del Rio children were there, although their grandparents weren't.

Mrs. Boyd, Helen and Ray's mother, had news for the boys and girls. She was a thin woman with brown hair that looked as if was dyed that color. She'd just stood up and said, "Boys and girls, we're going to do something that will be a great deal of fun."

"We're not going to plant petunias again, are we?" Joe asked. "I planted enough of those the last time."

"No, Joseph, we're not going to plant petunias. We're going to do something that will be good for you and good for your children."

"I don't have any children!" Jack Tanner said.

Everyone laughed, and Chili said, "I don't have any either. How many of you got children around here?"

"That's enough of that!" Mrs. White said. "Mrs. Boyd has a very good idea, and I want you to listen to her."

"Thank you, Mrs. White," Mrs. Boyd said. "Now, do any of you know who your great-great-grandparents were?" She looked around.

Only her own two children, Helen and Ray, were holding up their hands proudly.

"Well, that's a real shame. Every family ought to know about its roots. We call that knowing your family tree."

"I saw that on TV," Chili said. "Some black people went back to Africa and found out where they came from."

"That's exactly right. And I can trace the Boyd family all the way back to the *Mayflower*. One of my ancestors named Winslow was on the *Mayflower*. I was a Winslow until I married Mr. Boyd."

"Were there any Boyds on the *Mayflower*?" Flash asked.

"No. But we know about Mr. Boyd's family just as we know about my family. Now, what we are going to do is this: every one of you is going to find out as much as you can about your family."

"That doesn't sound like much fun," Jenny said. She rarely said anything at the meetings.

In seconds, most of the boys and girls were moaning and groaning.

But suddenly Juliet stood up. "Well, I think Mrs. Boyd has a good idea." She saw Mrs. Boyd look pleased at that. "I don't know much about my family. But I'd like to find out all I can. Wouldn't it be fun to find out that Buffalo Bill was your great-great-great grandfather?"

"Or maybe Billy the Kid," Jack Tanner said.

"I think it would be fun," Juliet insisted. She knew that there was one boy in the group who could talk anybody into anything, and that was Flash Gordon. She said, "Flash, don't *you* think it would be interesting to find out about your family?"

"I sure do," Flash said, "but I wouldn't know how to do it."

"Well, I know how to do it," Mrs. Boyd said. "And your family tree will be something that you can hand down to your children and grandchildren someday. Something you can be proud of."

When Flash joined in on Mrs. Boyd's side along with Juliet, it did not take long for the others to become interested.

After a while, Juliet said, "Delores, do you know who *your* ancestors were?"

"My grandparents do. We come from Spain."

Mrs. Boyd had been listening. "I think that's wonderful! I'd like to see your family tree. There were some real important people who came from Spain and settled in California and in Texas."

It was the first positive thing that Juliet had heard any of the Boyds say about the Del Rios. It made her feel good.

"Here's what we're going to do first," Mrs. Boyd said loudly. "I'm going to meet with your parents, all together at one time, and give them instructions on how to begin tracing your family trees."

"Is this going to cost a lot?" Mr. Tanner asked. "Some of us don't have a lot of money to spend on looking up a family tree."

"Don't worry about that. The costs are very small, and Mr. Boyd and I will be glad to help any who can't afford it."

"Good night!" Joe muttered. "I don't know what's got into Mrs. Boyd. She never gave anything away before."

"I'll tell you what it is," Juliet whispered back. "She's getting to do something that she's good at. I'll bet she knows everything about family trees."

Samuel was standing close enough to hear. "You really *want* to find out about who your ancestors were? Maybe some of them were bad."

"I'd like to know even if they were," Juliet said.

Joe nodded. "Yeah, we might be descended from a cattle rustler."

"I'll bet we're not," Juliet said. "I'll bet we're descendants of George Washington or somebody like that."

"Listen, Too Smart Jones," Joe said, "George Washington didn't have any children. Didn't you know that?"

Juliet blinked. "That's right. He didn't." She smiled at Joe, and said, "Thank you, Joe, for correcting me."

Joe seemed shocked that Juliet didn't blast off at him. She usually did when he caught her in a mistake. "Well," he said finally, still staring at her, "maybe something good will come out of this family tree business."

"I'll bet it does," Chili said. "I might find out that one of my ancestors was a king back in Africa. Then you'd have to call me Your Royal Highness."

Flash said, "Yeah, you just wait till I call you that." But he grinned.

Before long, the whole group began to get excited. Mrs. Boyd talked more about the meeting she would have with their parents. "And you boys and girls can come, too. You can all learn something from this."

Juliet and Joe were standing where they could hear Mrs. White and Mr. Tanner talking.

"I'm not sure I want to do this," Mr. Tanner was saying. "We may find out we're descended from the wrong people!"

"I'm sure you're not. You're too nice to come from a bad family."

Mr. Tanner took off his glasses and polished them. "That's one of the nicest things anyone ever said to me. I'm sure you come from a good family, too."

"Why don't we learn together? Why don't you come over for supper tonight? You can tell me all you know about your family, and we'll put it on my computer. Bring Jack too. He and Jenny can play together or watch TV while we're working."

"It sounds good to me. We'll be there."

"You see?" Juliet said softly to Joe. "They're falling in love."

"They're going to work on a family tree!" Joe snorted.

"You just wait and see. You'll find out."

10

Looking Back

This is one of the most fun things we've ever done, Joe." Juliet looked up from one of the sheets of paper scattered over their large worktable.

Juliet and Joe Jones were in the game room of their home. They had been working on their family tree. The table was cluttered with papers and several books. The stereo was playing one of the top songs by a Christian group.

"Yeah," Joe said. He picked up a sharpener and began to sharpen his pencil. "It's one thing you and I both like to work on."

"I guess that's because it's got lots of parts, like one of your inventions. And it's a mystery —the kind I like," Juliet said thoughtfully.

"It's a mystery all right. We don't know who we're going to come up with. We sure found out a lot about the family already."

"It was fun to find out that we had that senator from Mississippi in our family. Maybe we'll find a president if we keep on going. So it's sort of a mystery. But it's kind of like an invention too, Joe."

"How?"

"Well, I mean—when you invent something, you have to put together lots of little pieces to make the thing work. And that's what we're doing. Finding lots of little pieces about people. And people waste a lot of time inventing. Well, we spent all day yesterday looking for that part of our family that moved off to California. And we haven't found anything yet."

"But we will." Joe tightened his jaw. "We'll find them, or I'll bust."

The door opened, and their mother came in with a tray full of cookies and a big pitcher of something that looked good.

"What's that, Mom? Colored lemonade?" Joe asked.

"No. I'm out of lemons. This is cranberry juice."

"Cranberry juice! I don't like it."

"How can you say you don't like it," Juliet said, "when you haven't ever tasted it?"

"It doesn't look good."

"It looks beautiful," Juliet said. She poured herself a glass and took a sip. "Oh, it *is* good! Try it, Joe."

Joe hated to try anything new. He never

wanted to eat any ice cream but vanilla. He said that anybody who ate anything else was probably crazy. But he tasted the cold juice and smacked his lips. "Not bad," he said. He drained the glass, then said, "What kind of cookies are these?"

"Peanut butter pecan," their mother said. "They'll make you fat and pretty like me."

Juliet laughed. "You're pretty but you're not fat. I'll bet you never were."

"That's where you're wrong," Mrs. Jones said. "When I was just about your age, I was a very big girl."

"How did you stop being fat?" Joe stared at her in astonishment, as if he could not imagine his mother being an overweight ten-year-old.

"I just got older, and I also started watching what I ate. And when I married your father, he started me on all his fitness programs. So that's the secret, if there is one. How are you doing with the family tree?"

"Oh, it's going great, Mom. We've found out that those cousins we had back in the Civil War had big families. There were Joneses all over Tennessee."

"And one of them went North and fought on the Union side," Joe said. "And he was in General Grant's army. We found that out."

Mrs. Jones sat down with them. "I like to see you two working together like this. Usually you're trying to pull each other's hair out."

"It's just something Joe and I both like. It's real complicated, and Joe likes that. And there's a mystery about who we're going to find, and I like that. It's like a big jigsaw puzzle. But it's more fun than a jigsaw puzzle."

"I never did see why you liked jigsaw puzzles," Joe said. "You work and work on them, and then what have you got? A picture with lines all over it!"

"Did you ever finish that black one, Juliet?" her mom asked. It was a puzzle that was all black on both sides. There was no picture. When Juliet nodded, she said, "I don't see why you liked that one so much."

"Because it was hard," Juliet said. "When the picture's there, it's easy." That was true. Somehow she could pick up pieces that no one else could see and would put them right in place.

"Well, in any case I'm glad we're having peace. How far back are you going in the family tree?"

"All the way to Adam!" Joe cried.

"Well, maybe not that far," Juliet said. "But a ways. It's fun."

"I wonder how the others are doing?"

"We'll find out tomorrow. Everybody's supposed to bring their family trees to our meeting," Juliet said. "Mrs. Boyd is really excited."

"Well, it's been a good project. You've learned a lot about how to trace people. And you've found out about your own family."

"Some people in the world don't know who their parents are. They can't make a family tree. Aren't they kind of left out?" Joe asked.

"I don't think so," Juliet said quickly. "I think it's more important who *you* are than who your great-great-great grandfather was."

"And you're right, Juliet," their mother said, smiling. "Who you are and where you are with God. That's what counts."

Juliet thought the group meeting was very, very interesting today.

Mrs. Boyd was certainly enjoying herself. She showed slides of the Boyd and Winslow family trees. Then she talked about them.

"So we have twenty-seven college presidents in the Boyd family. And sixteen governors. And five senators," she said proudly. "And the Winslows—oh, there are so many important Winslows . . ."

She went on for a long time. But then she let one person from each family tell about his family tree.

Flash was so excited that he kept moving his wheelchair around. "We found out there are lots of preachers back in our family. One was a chaplain in General Washington's army during the Revolutionary War. Isn't that something?"

Both of Flash's parents were there. They seemed very proud of him.

"Flash is doing so well, Mrs. Gordon," Juliet's mother said.

"Yes. We're very proud of Melvin," Mrs. Gordon answered.

"And we're still praying that God's going to let him walk again," Mr. Gordon said. His eyes were misty as he looked at his son. Mr. Gordon worked as a bricklayer, but he preached every chance he got.

When Chili's turn came, his mother and father seemed proud of him, too. Chili said, "We're not real sure yet, but it looks like I'm gonna find out that my great-great-great granddaddy was a chief over in Africa." He grinned and nodded at his parents. "Mom and Dad, they say I can't be proud if that happens. But it wouldn't make me mad, either."

"That's fine, Roy," Mrs. Boyd said, giving Chili his real name. "I hope it turns out that you're exactly right."

One by one they went around the group until everyone had spoken.

"What about your other ancestors, Billy?" Jack Tanner asked. "You told us about the good ones, but how about that Rollins who got hung for horse stealing in Oklahoma?"

Juliet knew that Jack was not on good terms with Billy Rollins anymore. Jack said he didn't like the way that Billy made fun of the Del Rio children.

Billy Rollins said, "You shut up, Jack! I'll bet there are plenty of jailbirds in your family!"

Mr. Tanner said, "As a matter of fact, there was one well-known jailbird in *our* family."

Mrs. White turned instantly to look at him. "What jailbird is that, Loren?"

Mr. Tanner actually looked proud. "His name was John Bunyan."

"John Bunyan! You mean the man who wrote *Pilgrim's Progress?*" she gasped.

"That's the one. Bunyan was thrown in jail for preaching the gospel. He could have gotten out anytime he wanted to. He just had to say, 'I won't preach anymore.' But he never would do that. He spent more than ten years in a dirty prison while he had a big family outside that he couldn't help."

"I've always loved *Pilgrim's Progress,*" Mrs. White said. She was smiling broadly. "You must be very proud." Then she suddenly blushed and looked around. She must have forgotten that lots of people were listening.

"You see," Juliet whispered to Joe. "She likes him. She even likes his family."

"You're off your nut," Joe mumbled. But he looked over at Mr. Tanner and Mrs. White. "Well, he needs a helper all right," he muttered. "He can't remember to wear socks that match."

Mrs. Boyd was talking again. She said, "What we're going to do for the rest of this project is to write a paper about our families."

A big groan went up all over the room. Behind Juliet and Jenny, Jack Tanner moaned, "I can't ever do that."

Jenny turned around and looked at him. "Sure you can," she whispered back to him. "I'm good at writing stuff. I'll help you."

"Will you?"

"Sure I will. I'll get Mom to ask you and your dad back for supper. Then we can work on your paper."

Mrs. Boyd went on with her large plans. Now she was suggesting that the children could also make a family tree to hang up in their homes. It would remind them of who their families were.

The meeting was nearly over when Juliet heard the door open. She looked back to see Delores and Samuel Rio come in. They had almost missed the meeting. Quickly the two sat down in the back row.

"Oh, good!" Juliet said loudly. "Delores and Samuel are here. Did you find out anything about your family tree?"

"Yes," Delores said, but she did not stand up.

"But what did you find out? Who are your folks?" Flash asked.

Samuel and Delores looked at each other. Finally they seemed to agree. Samuel stood to his feet and said, "My grandfather has a letter from the king of Spain. It is to a lady named Del Rio."

"That's your name," Jack said.

"Yes. It was way back when Spain was very powerful—and the lady married the king of Spain."

There was total silence. And then Flash let out a yelp. "Good night! We've got a prince and a princess here and didn't even know it. Hooray for Prince Samuel and Princess Delores!"

Mr. Jones said, "Samuel and Delores, we've got to have your grandparents here to talk to us about your family!"

"We tried to get them to come, but they wouldn't," Delores said.

Flash whispered to Chili, "When they get those new clothes, they'll come to the next meeting. Won't they?"

"Sure they will. I'm real glad we got our parents into helping."

Billy Rollins was sitting with his head down and his lip stuck out. Flash felt sorry for him. He rolled his wheelchair over next to Billy and said, "Don't worry about it, Billy. All of us have *somebody* in our family that's done worse than stealing a horse. Looking back can be dangerous."

11

Mystery Solved

Juliet stood up and arched her back. She had been working on the family tree for two hours. She thought the display that she and Joe had made was beautiful.

Joe was a much better artist than she was, and he had drawn the family tree. It looked like a real tree turned upside down. At the top was the earliest family member that they had found. He was none other than John Paul Jones, the great naval hero.

"It looks good, doesn't it?" Joe said. He had just finished coloring the last of the tree, and he threw down the crayon. "We never did a better project. Imagine having an ancestor that was a *hero!*"

"Well, we've got more to do," Juliet said. "But it has been fun. The most fun has been looking at the old pictures. I'm glad that Mom and Dad got those pictures from Uncle Frank."

Uncle Frank lived in Pennsylvania. He had been keeping family pictures for years. He'd sent them, all carefully labeled. Juliet and Joe had found out about many of the people in their family.

"Well, have you finished writing, Juliet?"

"Just about. I want you to read it when I get through." They had agreed that Joe would do the drawing and Juliet would write the paper.

"Let's take a break and go over and see Samuel and Delores."

"Good idea. Mom's just baked a bunch of chocolate chip cookies, too," Juliet said. "We can take some over to them."

"Yeah, and maybe they'll have some enchiladas or something."

Twenty minutes later, Juliet and Joe were at the door of the old Del Rio house.

When they knocked, Delores opened it almost at once.

"We brought some chocolate chip cookies for you," Juliet said.

"Yeah. Have you got anything for us?" Joe asked.

"*Joe!* Don't be so impolite!"

"It's all right. My grandmother always has something cooking. Come in the house."

As usual, the Del Rio house smelled spicy

and fragrant. Mrs. Del Rio was standing at the stove. Samuel was in the kitchen, too.

She turned around and said, "Joe, I think you have radar. Every time there's food cooking, you seem to show up."

"I'm not dumb," Joe said, grinning. "I know to come where there's the best food in the world."

"Well, if you like apple pie, you've come to the right place. I've been baking all morning."

At that moment, Mr. Del Rio came in. He greeted Juliet and Joe warmly. "Did you tell them yet?" he asked, looking at his wife.

"Tell us what?" Juliet asked, puzzled.

Mrs. Del Rio beamed and said, "Let's not tell them. Let's show them. You wait right here and eat your pie."

As soon as the woman was out of the kitchen, Joe looked with bewilderment at Delores. "What's all this about?"

"It's a surprise."

"It is indeed a surprise—and a fine one," Mr. Del Rio said.

Mrs. Del Rio came back, holding two large boxes. She put them on the table and opened the tops. Reaching into one, she took out a dress, a beautiful powder blue dress. She held it up. "Isn't it beautiful?"

"It sure is," Juliet said. "That's the prettiest dress I've ever seen. You've been shopping."

Mr. Del Rio laughed. "No. We haven't been

shopping. But look at this." He opened the other box and took out a hangar that held a gray suit and a white shirt and tie. "Here, let me show you." He put on the coat. "Just a fit."

"You look gorgeous!" Juliet breathed. And he did. He was a fine-looking man anyway, but Juliet had never seen him in anything but worn clothing. "Where did you buy them?"

"We didn't buy them," he said. He smiled. "God sent them."

"How did He do that?"

"We have been praying for something new so that we could come to the meetings and go to church," Mrs. Del Rio said. "I know people didn't mind our old clothes, but I did. So we woke up this morning, and there the boxes were—out on the front porch."

"But who brought them?" Juliet asked.

"We don't know who God used to help us. Someone who has a good heart," Mr. Del Rio said. "Of course, we do not like to take from people, but someone went to a great deal of trouble . . ."

"Yes, they did. They got our sizes right and all." Mrs. Del Rio's eyes sparkled. "If you want a mystery to solve, Juliet, you can find out who left these clothes."

"Don't do it," Mr. Del Rio warned. "Whoever did it didn't want to be known. So we will thank the good Lord and pray that He will bless them."

"Go try on your dress, Mrs. Del Rio. I want to see it."

"And you put on your whole outfit, Mr. Del Rio," Joe said. "We don't want to wait to Sunday to see what it looks like."

"All right. We will do it," Delores's grandmother said. "Come along, Papa."

When the two left, Delores said, "It's so wonderful. They've bought new clothes for Samuel and me, but they haven't bought any for themselves in a long time. Don't they look wonderful?"

"They do! They really look great!" Juliet agreed.

"Well, come into the dining room. We'll show you some pictures of our family. Grandfather just got some in the mail from our uncle in Texas."

The big old dining room table was covered with pictures. Some were small black-and-whites, some were new and in color. Many were old and made of tin.

"We've got boxes of pictures we haven't even opened," Samuel said. His eyes danced. "It's nice having a king in the family. I feel better already."

"You'd make a good-looking king, Samuel," Joe told him. "And you'd be a beautiful princess, Delores."

They pulled out picture after picture and laughed at the old clothing and the old hairdos. Some of the pictures were paintings, not photographs.

Then Juliet picked up a large picture that was wrapped in a cloth. She carefully took off the covering, and it was a painting. Juliet stared at it and could hardly breathe. What she saw was a beautiful woman with dark hair and blue eyes. She was wearing a high-necked blouse with long sleeves. But Juliet was not thinking about that part. She whispered, "Look at this!"

"What?" Samuel asked.

He came up to stand on one side of Juliet. Delores came to the other side. Joe looked over her shoulder.

Juliet touched the painting. "That!"

There was silence for a moment. Then Joe said, "It's the necklace we found!"

They all began talking at once—loudly.

And at that moment Mr. and Mrs. Del Rio came in.

"What's the matter?" he asked. "Is something wrong?"

"Who is this woman, Grandfather?"

Mr. Del Rio took the painting and glanced at it. "Why, that is our great-great-grandmother, Maria Rosa Montez."

All of a sudden Juliet let out a shout. "Maria Rosa Montez! That's it! That's MRM! And that necklace she's wearing is the one that we found buried!"

Everyone was babbling, and no one was listening.

Finally Mrs. Del Rio said, "Quiet! Quiet, everyone!" When quiet was restored, she took the picture, saying, "How can this be? This is the same necklace, is it, Juliet?"

"Yes! See. A cross with diamonds. I'd know it anywhere."

Mr. Del Rio thought hard. Then he said, "I can only remember this faintly, but I can check it with my brother who lives in Mexico. When our grandfather bought this house years ago, we were only children. But I know there was a robbery, and many valuable things were stolen. The thief was never caught, and the jewelry was never found, and—"

"Well, it's found now," Juliet said. "Some of it, anyway. The mystery is solved."

"Not all of it," Samuel said. "Why would anybody bury jewels out there in the park? Why didn't they sell it?"

"We'll never find that out, I suppose," Juliet said. "Maybe they were almost caught and had to get rid of it in a hurry. Or maybe something else happened. But anyway, the big mystery is solved."

"We have to tell Chief Bender," Joe said.

The small office of Police Chief Bender seemed to be very full. Word had gotten around, and every spare inch was filled. People were even looking in through the windows.

The chief looked at the painting that Mr. Del Rio handed him. Then he looked at the necklace that he had taken out of his safe. "There's no doubt about it," he said. "This is the same necklace. And you, Mr. and Mrs. Del Rio, are the rightful owners." He handed over the box of jewelry.

Juliet cheered with everyone else. Then she grabbed Delores in a hug, and Joe hugged Samuel.

"What are you going to do with all the money just that necklace will bring? We got an appraisal on it. It's worth a lot of money," the chief said.

"I think we've already decided that," Mr. Del Rio said slowly. "We asked God to let us stay in my family home right here in Oak-wood. And now He has made it possible."

"That is right," his wife said. "We'll spend the rest of our days here. And you, Delores, and you, Samuel, will have a better life."

"Can I still be a flyer someday?" Samuel asked.

"I don't know whether God wants that for you or not," his grandfather said. "Circus life is very hard. But whatever He wants, we have good Christian friends to help us. Don't we, Mama?"

Mrs. Del Rio held the necklace up against

her throat. "Yes," she whispered, and tears came to her eyes. "We have good friends. And we have a good detective—Miss Jones—who has helped us keep our family together."

Juliet's throat was full. She could not say a word. She felt tears come into her own eyes.

And then Delores threw her arms around Juliet, and everyone cheered again.

12

The Party

Joe stood staring around the Del Rios' front yard. Before, it had been full of weeds and trash. Now it was perfectly clear. New grass was growing. Flowers grew in all of the beds, and the house itself gleamed with white paint. It had a Spanish look with the little towers on top. The roof was new and blue, and everything sparkled.

"I wouldn't have believed it," Juliet said. "It looks beautiful. And it couldn't have happened to nicer people."

"Let's go around back. I hear music."

When they arrived at the backyard, they found that most of the support group youngsters and their parents were already there. The smell of cooking hamburgers was in the air.

Joe said, "There's Dad. He's helping barbecue. I'm starved. Let's see if we can get a sample."

The Del Rios stood off by themselves, smiling and watching. They were wearing their new clothes—no one had found out who had left them.

When it came time for Mr. Del Rio to make a speech, he said, "Thank you for coming to help us move into our new house. A 'housewarming,' I think you call it. The clothes, also, we thank you for," he said, "although we do not know who gave them. But whoever did such a deed has a kind heart."

"Let's have a speech from you too, Mrs. Del Rio," Juliet's mother said. She went over and gave the woman a hug. "Welcome to your old home and your new home."

Mrs. Del Rio said, "Thank you so much. You're all so kind." She almost began to cry but dashed her tears away. "How can I say what is in my heart? Here, after many years, we have found people who love us. Samuel and Delores have found friends who care for them. And Ramon and I, in our later years, have found a safe place for the rest of our journey."

There was quiet then in the backyard. No one seemed to know what to say.

And then Mr. Rollins stood up. He cleared his throat. Everyone stared at him. He and his wife had been sitting apart from everyone else, and both looked totally uncomfortable.

"I've got one thing to say," Mr. Rollins said. He cleared his throat again, then walked over to the Del Rios. "This is hard for me, but I've got to say it." He tried to speak, then shook his head. "I'm pretty good at talking, but there are two words that I can't say easily. The words 'I'm sorry.'"

A murmur went over the group. Juliet dug her elbow into Joe's ribs. He immediately gave her a dig back.

"But I *am* sorry. And I want everybody to hear me say it," Mr. Rollins said. "I said some mean things about you folks, and I was totally wrong. I'll have to ask you to forgive me—if you will."

Immediately Mr. Del Rio stepped forward and put out his hand. His wife hugged Mrs. Rollins.

"That makes the day perfect," Juliet said.

"Except for Billy. Look at him. He looks like a lost cause," Joe said.

"Let's go see if we can cheer him up."

"He's a rat, but he's our rat," Joe agreed.

Juliet said, "Hi, Billy."

"Hello."

Billy Rollins did not even lift his eyes.

Joe said, "After we get some of this food down, why don't you, and me, and Juliet, and the Del Rios—and any of the rest of the kids that want to—go fishing over in the creek?"

"They wouldn't want me," Billy said.

"Well, *I* want you," Juliet said.

Billy Rollins looked up then. To Juliet's amazement, he said, "I've been rotten."

"You sure have," Joe said. He put an arm around Billy. "But we're all rotten sometimes."

Juliet put her arm around him, too. "You should know some of the rotten things *I've* done."

"Not you two."

"That's what you think," Juliet said. "Now, come on. How about it? Let's go get some of that food they're dishing out."

They pulled at Billy and finally got him to the table. And there stood Samuel and Delores, watching.

"Go on, Billy," Juliet whispered, "say it. You'll feel better."

He gave her a surprised look. "How'd *you* know what I was thinking?"

"I just know because I've felt the same way. More than once."

"You're too smart," Billy mumbled. But then he straightened up and said, "Hey, I'm sorry about being mean to you guys."

It was the only apology that anyone had ever heard Billy Rollins make.

At once Samuel and Delores smiled at him. "That's all right, Billy," Delores said. "Everybody's wrong sometimes. Now, come over here, and I'll see that you get the biggest enchilada you ever saw in your life."

Juliet watched Delores haul Billy off. Billy, she noticed, did not take much urging.

"Well, that's a miracle if I ever saw one," Joe said.

At that moment Mrs. White called, "May I have your attention before we eat?"

Everyone turned to look.

And suddenly Mr. Tanner was standing beside her. He looked around and seemed somewhat embarrassed. "We have an announcement to make," he said.

He never got to make the announcement because Juliet screamed, "You and Mrs. White are going to get married!"

"Juliet, you hush!" her mother said.

"It's all right," Mr. Tanner said. "That's what I was going to say. Vicki and I love each other, and we're going to marry sometime soon. Jack approves of her as his mother. And I've got Jenny's approval to try and be the best dad I can be to her."

Jack Tanner and Jenny then joined their parents, and the four of them stood together, smiling, while people clapped.

Juliet once again poked Joe in the ribs. "See? I solved the mystery of the buried treasure, and I knew Mr. Tanner and Mrs. White would get married."

Joe stared at her. "Too Smart Jones, you're in for a fall. You're getting too proud."

Juliet was tired, for the party at the Del Rios had lasted for a long time. At last, though, the Joneses were home and getting ready for bed.

Juliet went down to the kitchen to get a drink of water. When she came back, she found Joe standing outside her door. "What's the matter?"

"Nothing," Joe said, spreading his hands apart. "I just wanted to tell you what a good sister you are."

Juliet gaped at him. She could not believe he was saying such a nice thing.

But then he smiled. And Joe had a world-class smile.

She said, "Well, thank you, Joe. And I want to tell you you're a wonderful brother."

"We make a good team," Joe said. "Good night. I hope you sleep well."

Juliet said, "Thank you, Joe, and I hope you have a good night, too."

Juliet put on her pajamas and prayed and turned out the light. Slipping under the covers, she felt very tired. "Bet I sleep good tonight," she said to herself. "I'll sleep good and—"

Suddenly her feet touched something cold and wet—and alive! She let out a piercing scream.

Juliet scrambled out of the bed. She fell onto the floor and kept on screaming. Then she jumped up and turned the light back on.

She threw back the covers—and saw a large, green bullfrog.

It said, *"Grumph!"*

At once Juliet straightened up. "I'll kill you, Joseph Jones!" she cried. She ran to the door, opened it, and headed for Joe's door.

She found him doubled over with laughter. "Have you seen my friend Hector? I can't seem to find him. It's a mystery where he's gone."

"I'll fix you, Joe!" Juliet jumped on him and began punching.

Joe fended off her blows, but he could not stop laughing. Finally he cried out, "Don't hit me anymore. It's a mystery who put that frog in there. You love a mystery, Too Smart Jones. So solve it!"

Dixie Morris Animal Adventures

3363-4 Dixie and Jumbo
3364-2 Dixie and Stripes
3365-0 Dixie and Dolly
3366-9 Dixie and Sandy
3367-7 Dixie and Ivan
3368-5 Dixie and Bandit
3369-3 Dixie and Champ
3370-7 Dixie and Perry
3371-5 Dixie and Blizzard
3382-3 Dixie and Flash

Follow the exciting adventures of this animal lover as she learns more of God and His character through her many adventures underneath the Big Top.
Ages 9-14

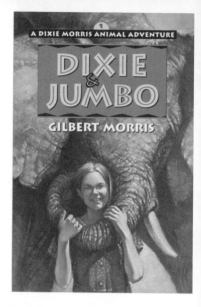

The Daystar Voyages

4102-X Secret of the Planet Makon
4106-8 Wizards of the Galaxy
4107-6 Escape From the Red Comet
4108-4 Dark Spell Over Morlandria
4109-2 Revenge of the Space Pirates
4110-6 Invasion of the Killer Locusts
4111-4 Dangers of the Rainbow Nebula
4112-2 The Frozen Space Pilot
4113-0 White Dragon of Sharnu
4114-9 Attack of the Denebian Starship

Join the crew of the Daystar as they traverse the wide expanse of space. Adventure and danger abound, but they learn time and again that God is truly the Master of the Universe.
Ages 10-14

MOODY
The Name You Can Trust
1-800-678-8812 www.MoodyPress.org

Get swept away in the many Gilbert Morris Adventures available from Moody Press:

"Too Smart" Jones

4025-8 Pool Party Thief
4026-6 Buried Jewels
4027-4 Disappearing Dogs
4028-2 Dangerous Woman
4029-0 Stranger in the Cave
4030-4 Cat's Secret
4031-2 Stolen Bicycle
4032-0 Wilderness Mystery
4033-9 Spooky Mansion
4034-7 Mysterious Artist

Come along for the adventures and mysteries Juliet "Too Smart" Jones always manages to find. She and her other homeschool friends solve these great adventures and learn biblical truths along the way. Ages 9-14

Seven Sleepers - The Lost Chronicles

3667-6 The Spell of the Crystal Chair
3668-4 The Savage Game of Lord Zarak
3669-2 The Strange Creatures of Dr. Korbo
3670-6 City of the Cyborgs
3671-4 The Temptations of Pleasure Island
3672-2 Victims of Nimbo
3673-0 The Terrible Beast of Zor

More exciting adventures from the Seven Sleepers. As these exciting young people attempt to faithfully follow Goél, they learn important moral and spiritual lessons. Come along with them as they encounter danger, intrigue, and mystery. Ages 10-14

Moody Press, a ministry of the Moody Bible Institute, is designed for education, evangelization, and edification. If we may assist you in knowing more about Christ and the Christian life, please write us without obligation: Moody Press, c/o MLM, Chicago, IL 60610.